THE NONCONFORMIST PLEA-BARGAIN

Matthew Lotti

ISBN-10: 0-9715594-0-6
ISBN-13: 978-0-9715594-0-0

Library of Congress Control Number: 2001119973

Cover Design by John A. Simone.

For Theresa Kolman, my grandmother

"You know, it is an extraordinary thing in life to be anonymous - not to be famous or great, not to be very learned, not to be a tremendous reformer or revolutionary, just to be nobody; and when one really feels that way, to be suddenly surrounded by a lot of curious people creates a sense of withdrawal."

- J. Krishnamurti

1.

It is Thursday morning, 7:15 AM, and I'm sitting uncomfortably in a cold, plastic booth in a generic fast food restaurant that specializes in breakfast and has been spreading locally like pollen. I don't know why I chose to come here, but I did and here I sit. On the ugly, stained table in front of me is my breakfast: three flapjacks coated in "real" maple syrup, three sausage links, three burnt strips of bacon, a scoop of grits and a piping hot cup of slightly burnt decaffeinated coffee, blended with two creams and two sugars to kill the taste. My booth is in the far corner of the room - trying to avoid most everyone else - with my back to the outside window. From my position I can see everything, which is my intention. At the counter, there are construction workers buying the same kinds of foods I bought for myself they clearly do not need. Seated nearby are some senior citizens, usually in packs and chatting old-people prattle (regarding old times and other people and grizzly ailments) over lukewarm tea in Styrofoam cups. In the opposing corner are clean-shaven businessmen - two to be precise - wolfing down their egg, cheese and green pepper omelets and coffee, while simultaneously reading their newspapers while simultaneously monitoring their shiny-but-cheap watches to see how quickly they have to eat while simultaneously looking up every time someone new walks in while occasionally glancing in the direction of the blonde teenage (19?) girl working the one and only register, who they ordered from, and who is now waiting on some semi-handicapped 40-something with his mother/caretaker who can't seem to make up his mind as to whether or not he wants a sausage roll or French Vanilla flavored waffles. It's a good thing I'm not behind him in line, as I would grow unabashedly impatient and uncharacteristically verbal and yell, "Pick one! They'll both kill you!"

Oh: as for why I'm in a fast food restaurant. I had one hell of a hard time falling asleep last night - it felt like it was in the high-90's and I couldn't seem to relax or get settled when I was pouring sweat from every orifice, an uncomfortable state most people find themselves in when doing battle with a virus. Conveniently, there is no central air in my apartment building, and I do not have one of those two hundred pound microwave-sized portable ones to wedge in a window. Therefore, I arose this morning at 6-something, with another two hours left to waste, showered and left early to hang out and relax here. I realized then that these cold, awkward, plastic booths were actually carefully designed (by either psychologists or psychiatrists, I think) to provide *little* comfort for your body, as a friendly sort of *push* to get you to eat and leave as quickly as you can, without unnecessary dawdling or lounging. If you want to lounge, they're saying, silently, do it someplace else, like an actual restaurant or your local church. But I wasn't in the mood for either of those, and really just wanted a cup of coffee. I ordered the pancakes (which I have no desire to touch) out of custom.

In forty some minutes - I check my Fossil watch - I have to be at "work." As for what to say about work, I'm rather at a loss. It is a giant health insurance corporation that employs a vast array of people of all shapes and colors and the like, all from different backgrounds and cultures and races and creeds (or, at least, that's what all the newspaper ads about it have said). I think it's fantastic that a company can be so diversified and still work as a whole (or at least create such an illusion).

My position, that of a "Claims Analyst," is both painfully redundant and sickeningly easy - so easy the majority of the people in the world could do it, once they get the gist of the job's requirements and how to use the most basic functions on a computer. Yet, I admit to not being thrilled with being called a "Claims Analyst," a rather dull title, and, when asked by others outside of work what I do, tell them I'm an "Administrative Technological Consultant," although truth be told I have absolutely no clue as to what all of those words mean, and have no idea as to whom they might actually apply, so it's essentially a private joke that's not exactly funny. One would assume that considering what type of personality I have I would savor the redundancy, but it's quite the contrary - I oppose redundancy not created by me and not doing what I want to do. I am not the type of person who requires constant amusement via the infinite forms of entertainment available on the market, nor do I need every day to be 20th Century Fox. If I personally were running the show, I would most likely go fucking ape shit for the sake of my fellow co-workers and their amusement. The following would be constructed for their benefit: a library for carefree reading, "viewing chambers" - small rooms with television sets to watch mid-day soap-operas, "listening chambers" for audio pleasure (complete with most every assortment of music available except opera and hard rock, not because I disapprove of them, but because neither are 'relaxing'), "massage chambers" with trained masseuses for occasional backrubs, rub downs, jerk-offs and "scent chambers" in which fine fragrances ooze into plain looking rooms. And, if the state will bend to my will, I would love to install an "opium chamber" with beds covered in satin, small tables burning candles, dim lighting and soft violin music playing oh-so-sweetly in the background. Alas, how silly of me!

Such things would never fly. I can hardly run a lawnmower much less a multi-million-billion dollar company with X number of employees and Y number of acres of corporate land space and Z tasks to accomplish. Of course I *realize* that one couldn't run a business with all the aforementioned luxuries though I do enjoy brainstorming sometimes.

7:35. Time is moving slowly. My focus has now switched from myself (gratefully) to the girl working the cash register. I'm not close enough to her to get a crystal clear look at her face - but I predict she's either 18 or 19, probably just out of high school. I don't recall what her eyes looked like from when I was in line with her to order my meal, as I take special precaution to completely avoid establishing eye-contact with most people I encounter, male or female, black or white. The female has auburn hair that's hanging out of the back (and sides, especially over the ears) of the bright red hat she has on.

I wonder what a girl her age - who is attractive (according to current social standards) and seemingly bright - is doing right here, right now, working for minimum wage. What mistakes did she make or people make for her that has her end up in such a place. Is it a part-time endeavor? Will she depart in six months? I say "seemingly bright" because I don't have the Stanford-Binet test on me to assess her intellectual prowess. I question whether or not she comes from a broken home, a history of mental problems, takes medication, is poor or what. I question exactly how and why she isn't working at ... oh ... a bank, for instance, or a grocery store, or as a secretary at a law firm. I wonder if she has a boyfriend, a husband and many friends. I watch her move - she seems relatively cheerful and comfortable waiting on people. She doesn't have that "newbie" look on her face that telegraphs utter confusion or panic - she knows what to get where and where to go if what she wants is not there, leading me to assume she's been doing this a while (not that it requires excessive mental strain).

I notice that the businessmen have since left as have the old ladies. The indecisive man and his eating partner are seated in the center of the room at a table for two. It is unclear which menu option they settled for.

7:48. It is almost time to leave. I don't like showing up on time *exactly*. In fact - I don't like showing up on time *anywhere*. While in college, when I went to class, I had created for myself a rule in which I could neither be:

a.) one of the first three people seated in class nor
b.) more than 2 minutes early.

If I showed up for a 2:10 class at 2:06 and there was only one person seated, I would run to the bathroom to wash up or examine myself in the mirror, take a self-guided tour of the rest of the building, reading the dry intellectual jokes on the doors of the professors' offices or grab a carbonated drink at a nearby vending machine, taking my time opening it, and then saunter about aimlessly, all the while keeping a close eye on my watch. Once it hit 2:11 I strolled into class, assured there would be more people seated and waiting. For some strange reason I was always preoccupied with being early or on-time as I never wanted anyone to think I was eager to hear the lecture or had nothing better to do with my time.

7:53. After recognizing the dull irony of my sitting in such an environment and giving it so much attention and sad thought, I dispose of the balance of my breakfast and walk out the door.

2.

I usually find myself at work around 8:15 or 8:20, though I do not fear reprimands for lateness because no one pays any attention to me. At least once a week I try to stop in and talk to Preston, the Security Guard, who has a tiny little office to the right of the main entrance, in the atrium. Preston, I have found, likes baseball and sports just as much as I do, and follows it obsessively, often going to games and the like.

However, since we owe allegiance to different teams (him Florida, me Philadelphia) we usually don't discuss that as much as we ruminate on random things, most of which lead back to him - his wife, his son, his vacation plans, etc. Most conversations start off with a "how are you," from him, but quickly turn around into something like "I'm glad you're fine, now let's document extensively how *I* am doing," giving me little room to fill in the blank. Everyone does this, however - reverts all stories back to themselves - so he's hardly to blame. *We all speak in monologues, there is little discussion.*

I peek in the door and give a wave.

He looks up and at his watch. "Twenty minutes again! If I were your boss I don't think I'd put up with this." He takes his feet off the desk and tosses down the Money section of the USA Today.

"If you were my boss I'd demand a raise and an office."

"How are you today? You look down."

"You know. It's the morning. How's the, how's your son?"

He flicks at a button on his white short-sleeve shirt to remove an errant string that was stuck on it. "You know what Kyle did on ... what was it ... Friday? Thursday? No ... no, it was Friday. He and one of his friends were chasing after this little girl and her friends with tennis rackets. Now I didn't know what was going on - I'm inside watching the Mets. Anyway, next thing I know, I get this girl's father ringing my door bell, banging on the front door, yelling obscenities, and the guy, he completely startles me, and I told him I had no idea what's going on and he says his daughter got hit in the face but my kid says no and...."

"Did he?"

"I guess, I, I think he was just playing. I think it was an accident. I don't know."

"Did he warn you? You know, make demands?"

"He just said to keep my kid away from her and, of course, you know Kyle has a different story."

"Like, the girl fell on the tennis racket."

He shakes his head. "So now he's grounded. What else can I do?"

"Not much," I say, "but then again, I don't know what anyone else could do either. He's a kid."

I proceed to the elevator, press the up-arrow button and wait for it to come down. When it opens, Mr. Thomas is inside. Mr. Thomas (first name I can't recall) is always leisurely dressed despite having such a lofty position as Head of the Something. It's not uncommon to see him in Hawaiian or polo shirts, T-shirts with logos on them, and, in the wintertime, jeans and pullover sweatshirts. He's always been unusually kind to me (perhaps because we both went to the same college, different years) going out of his way to say high, or wave or smile, which I return with a smile of my own.

He's talking on his cell phone but still looks up and nods as he walks past me towards the entrance and out, his sandals sliding silently over the marble floor.

I find my way to my desk/workstation and sit down and begin sifting through the files that seems to have collected in the metal bin that holds my work. No one approaches me, tells me I'm late, leaves seething notes in large print indicating I'm being docked time and money or anything of the sort. No one wishes me a 'good morning.' Honestly, I'm not really sure anyone's ever around.

There's a computer at the desk that never works properly and is outdated and the keyboard is all black and full of grime. I keep forgetting to bring my bottle of Windex from home to wipe up the place as the cleaning crew does a careless job but I don't leave angry notes demanding they take action - some workers in some companies in some places have this most disgusting habit of leaving detailed notes about "Wiping this up" or "Remove this pile of" papers or files, usually followed by exclamation marks suggesting furious anger. I never pick on the cleaning crew as I was, for all three years of high school, employed by OfficeClean. Likewise, my peers, at the time, all had out-of-school jobs to make extra money to buy cars and music and such - Patrick worked at FoodPlace and Michele at Jerry's Luncheon and George at ThriftPlus. I didn't want to work and slave and toil, but my parents - true bastions of understanding and emotional cushioning - suggested strongly that I find something like *those others*. They insisted I work for OfficeClean, because they knew one of the bosses there, and I, as a result of my own foolish decision-making (had I been smarter I would have made a decision before they made theirs), would end up cleaning bathrooms and dusting desks and shelves and vacuum the floors of businesses in the area, after they closed. OfficeClean would usually send two people to each job to ease the burden (some of these complexes were large and required a lot of maintenance from a lot of cleaning people).

For my duration I worked with a plethora of people ranging from the relatively young (mid-twenties) to old (late-fifties), educated to uneducated. There was one man, however, who I spent a good deal of time with - a 40-something year old Encyclopedia Salesman by the name of Chet. Chet was severely balding (you could count the strands), short (but thin) and wore thick, tinted chestnut-colored glasses. He once told me how Chet was actually a nickname he warranted in his younger days when he played the trumpet and idolized Chet Baker. Chet's real name was Daniel, but that was also his father's name, and he disliked being called "Danny Boy."

I once asked him if he still played.

"Nah. I keep it someplace in the basement, in its case, collecting dust. There was one day when I realized I could never play as well as I wanted to - when I didn't have that 25% *extra* talent that I needed. I have never touched it since. It's a shame, really, how that happens to you - I know it's happened to others - where you just aren't given what others are, and the whole dream crumbles. You move on."

Chet was, in my opinion, a rather downbeat person, although I'm not sure it had to do *entirely* with his musical proficiency (or lack thereof). I looked at it as a combination of several factors: bad divorce, custody battle (he lost), bad day job and filthy night job. A predisposition to being downbeat could fit in there as well.

Chet was a perfectionist when we would clean. He would insist on doing the vacuuming and dusting parts (leaving me - conveniently - with the bathrooms and trash elimination) and would methodically cleanse every single horizontal shelf, desk or filing cabinet with the utmost care. It would take him forever to run the vacuum cleaner over the carpets as he would stop every couple of minutes to get on his hands and knees to hand-pick staples out of the carpet that the Hoover couldn't consume. He would arrange the objects on the desks in obsessively neat piles, and straighten out the stacks of papers. I found this grating for one reason and one reason only: the OfficeClean job was just that - a job - and if you honestly wish to be such a way you should stick to doing it at home on your own time. I wanted to shake his tiny little frame senseless, as it would get late (we never got paid for overtime) and I wanted so desperately to get home.

But despite his faults I always felt he was an honest enough man, and never treated me in a derogatory fashion or belittled me, perhaps because he saw potential in me, perhaps because that was simply 'his way.' He would often recant for me stories of his own youth over Instant Coffee in the break room/cafeteria we were working at. During my senior year in high school, I discussed - at length - my college surveying with Chet. He, not so much interested in me as in dredging up memories of his own past, told me how he got into a fraternity, lived in this dorm with these types of people, first day jitters, problems with professors and his eccentric friends (that he'd lost touch with shortly after graduation). I don't recall which school he went to, but I believe he graduated in music, which he naturally called his "big mistake," and when I mentioned he could try graduate studies he simply hemmed and hawed and made excuses.

———

Today, at work, I get all of my "assignments" completed, so by 4:00 I have an hour to waste until I am permitted to leave. I never know if what I do on these tasks I get handed are correct or not, and no one ever stops by to tell me "This is good" or "You missed something here." The majority of what I do consists of sifting through claims people submit to the insurance agency, and process them in the computer, punching information into the company's system regarding the doctor's information, the dates of service, procedures performed, the doctor's diagnoses, reimbursements, premiums, deductibles and a million other things I'd rather not go on about. If the forms are not completed, or have missing information, I'm supposed to make phone calls to get the proper information, though most often I simply toss the papers away in the brown plastic waste can under my desk/workstation, figuring that if *you*, the person submitting the claim were that fucking concerned with your own health, you'd take the time to put the proper information on the forms without forcing me to get on the phone and get your date of birth or annual salary or Social Security number. I have a strong aversion towards/distrust of telephones and would rather not use them.

3.

Tonight's dinner back at my apartment is a frozen chicken patty with a side of wild rice and a glass of tap water. For dessert: an orange-flavored multi-vitamin and a cup of green tea. My apartment - located on Riverside Lane on the South Side of my hometown, is actually quite nice and clean considering the monthly $400 price tag (a steal). There are two other tenants in this building - a nice girl named Amy on the first floor and a fellow named Seth on the second. Neither Seth nor Amy speak to me much - perhaps twice a year we chat or make idle conversation but it never amounts to much. I've only been living here for two years or so, while Seth and Amy have been here considerably longer. Apparently the girl who used to live in my apartment was a vicious she-devil (and stereotypical bad tenant) named Clara or Claire or Clarissa or Clementine or whatever and she would play her dance-trance-techno bass-slamming clamor at the most obscene times - around three or four in the morning - causing sleep and general thinking disturbances in both Seth and Amy, who both were trying oh-so-hard to live out their existences in relative silence. The times I would speak to either of them they would usually end up on the subject of 'this girl' (I'll stick to calling her "Clara" because her hair reminds me a smidge of Clara Bow's) and how loud she was and how quiet I am and what-a-blessed-relief because wow, what a total pain in the ass, and did I tell you about the time she hit her boyfriend with a lamp or had the police come in droves on numerous occasions and at the most inopportune times and how fantastic it is that she moved to Illinois or Wisconsin because whew, we thought we'd have to move first.

The little I know about each: Amy is currently employed at Foodstuffs, where she's currently the manager. She told me that she "finds meeting people exciting," which is why she's stayed there so many years. I'm positive she never went to college, and struggled out of high school ("Too busy having fun and not focusing"), ran off for a while with her then-boyfriend (whose name eludes me) who drove a truck and "thought he was a rock star." Anyway, those little teenage love-fests never last, and he, like the rolling stone he is/was, "found another floozie and took off" (her words). This sent her for a loop - she tried out community college, couldn't stick with it, left and worked two jobs to make ends meet.

Amy's about 29-30 now and while I don't mean to be rude isn't exactly the most stunning individual you'd ever meet - she's a tad homely and wears absolutely no makeup whatsoever, has sloppy fashion sense (T-shirts from amusement parks, cut-offs, baseball caps), but I swear she has the nicest smile I've ever seen. It's almost perfect: the rounded lips, the delicate curves, the pure white, clean, parallel, even teeth. I never asked whether or not she had work done on them or if they're caps or anything like that, and how often she brushes, or flosses or uses bleaching mouthwash or if she had them bleached by a dentist.

I know considerably less about pointy-chinned Seth, who, instead of mostly speaking of himself, mostly does his own thing. Seth and I are only connected in two ways: 1.) he's always going on vacations - I'd approximate one every three months - and whenever he goes he asks me to take care of his cat Capo, which I agree to, begrudgingly and 2.) outside my apartment door there's a small, vacant, dingy storage closet that I don't use and he asked me if I could be so kind to let him keep his Cannondale bicycle in since I'm not using it. He never quite explained why he couldn't keep it in his own apartment or someplace else, but it's really not important.

All in all I can never say I really "know" either of these two people because I've never, for example, eaten a meal with them or gone on a trip with them. I find these two criteria to be of the utmost importance in getting to know someone. Although it takes more than a meal and a vacation to get a good sense of where an individual stands on certain issues, his or her hobbies/interests or general temperament, it is a good start. I find that I can't share a meal with someone I don't know especially well and may not like or be wary of. For me to eat with someone, I have to be comfortable *to a fault* around him or her.

As for me and my eating habits: I fear that my inability to cook anything elaborate is a severe liability. For one to dine alone - as I've always tried to do - it's best to have some sort of sense how to make basic things. Other than eggs and pasta I'm fairly clueless (and I avoid eggs due to extremely high levels of cholesterol - over 70% per egg). The chicken breast I'm eating tonight is so simple to make a 10-year-old could prepare it, if he/she were attentive and willing, yet as I examine the packaging I notice that the fat and saturated fat content (not to mention the sodium) are all mighty high - too high for someone that comes from a family just waiting for heart disease to strike. Granted, I am nowhere near middle age, and in relatively good health, but it's good to start early, I think.

I tried to get my mother to teach me how to make steak or stew or stir fry or shish-ka-bobs or soup (I drool over the thought of French Onion) but for some reason she and I never got around to doing it ("I have no faith in my own lousy cooking," she would say, "I shouldn't be the one to show you"). In particular, I needed some assistance with a white wine gazpacho recipe some years back - I found the

recipe in a battered copy of *Good Housekeeping* or *Ladies'*
Home Journal or some other woman-based magazine that I
leafed through while at one of several doctor's offices long
ago - and loved the picture of the finished product and the
article that accompanied it. Apparently the woman who
had written the piece had wonderful memories of having
the soup for the first time. She told about how an old
boyfriend had cooked for her on her birthday as a surprise.
The gazpacho was actually the appetizer - the main dish
was some elaborate chimichanga-type fried something.
She went on to talk about how he left her or contracted
cancer or something sweeping and dramatic like that, but it
was the gazpacho - that cold Mexican soup - that reminded
her of him and that magical night and the way his after-
shave tingled her nose and the glimmer of the light on his
visage, sparked by a myriad of candles spread all around
the room and the lush sounds of a Cocteau Twins album
that played softly and sweetly in the magical room. But I
did save the recipe - and the article. Perhaps I am, deep
down, a closet romantic?

Anyhow, Mom basically left me high and dry in terms
of culinary knowledge, so I've been surviving by making
either microwaveables or pasta or simple, simple things.
Due to my inborn laziness I don't bother going to a
bookstore to buy some kind of how-to book.

Most nights are spent, reading or listening to the radio or
sitting on the balcony affixed to my apartment and
watching others pace about below. I try to take time to
write thoughts down and attempt to maintain a journal of
personal goals, wishes, anecdotes and feelings, and keep
them in the massive gray filing cabinet that I got from Dad
(who replaced his with newer, less dented-and-banged up
models). I kept a journal in college and filled it full of
thoughts and words and confessions - mostly confessions -
all of which positively frighten me when I read them today,
although I'm not sure why they should. I actually feel

guilty and pathetic and weak for having written them, and this 'strangeness' compels me to throw them away. I had an entire journal, some 300 pages, when I was in high school, that was chock full of observations regarding peers, family, life, everything. But one weekend I had nothing to do and was alone in the house and became enraged, while re-reading some of them, and set the journal on fire by throwing the pages, piecemeal, into the furnace of my home. I watched as the words and pages turned into soot before my eyes, and disappeared, without a trace, and became nothing, and I felt quite relieved, actually, because I didn't - and wouldn't - want anyone to find them and read them and come to immediate conclusions. I swore, that day, to never make another journal ... but in time I violated my own rule. I need to write, to sketch, to create idiotic collages as some sort of personal therapy. Everyone needs to let it out in some way.

Anyway, I kept this college journal, all the scraps of papers and notes and organized them (and various other snippets of information, doodles and the like) in the filing cabinet. For this apartment I have essentially tried to back away from the scattered disorganization of my college years, and opted for a simpler, cleaner approach that cuts down on the trash and chaos and disorder. As you enter the front door you see the kitchen, with the stove and microwave and sink. In the middle sits the kitchen table. To the left, a storage closet, where I keep unused junk. Walk in further, and you'll see the wall-to-wall dressers for clothing storage, a vanity mirror, the filing cabinet pressed against a rectangular divider that cuts the room in two parts, one ¾, the other ¼, the ¼ section being the bedroom; since I've grown so accustomed to it, my mattress is directly on the floor, and next to it, a single dresser with a small ceramic lamp one of my aunts made. Adjacent to the "bedroom" section is the bathroom, with a shower and sink.

All the walls and ceiling are bare, unmarked by notes or obscure drawings or paintings or framed anything (I no longer have the maps of the continents and countries I had while in my college dorm - I left them up). However, there is still a noted absence of any computer equipment, television, advanced technological equipment hogging the electrical outlets (my phone and my radio - which was given to me by acquaintance Davis one Christmas - are the only things worth stealing).

I shower after washing up the dishes for about an hour, then go out on the balcony with the radio on low (playing some morose bass-driven jazz piece with a Latin name) and sit and relax, sipping ice water from my Garfield mug. The night breeze blows the baby blue bathrobe I'm wearing slightly, and it feels delicious as it relocates the hairs on my legs. Being Tuesday, it's peaceful and serene and unassuming beneath me. On a usually popular Riverslide Lane there are only two cars to be seen parked on the narrow street. It's 9:30 PM and I'm guessing others are winding down as well. The quiet allows me time to think.

4.

Last night I kept the sliding balcony door slightly ajar, to allow some air to enter the moist room, and allow me to get a good night's rest (I lost consciousness at 11-ish, granting me eight decent hours of serenity). However, the night never quite seems long enough, and I find myself back at work. While lounging, and giving my head a rest, I decide, impulsively, to start sifting through the local papers for any potential job opportunities in the area.

My rationale: change in lifestyle.

One tends to get set in one's ways. Then, one day, one decides to simply change his or her outlook. Mine's out of a combination of boredom and curiosity. What else is there to do?

During my lunch hour, I walked to the local FastStop and bought today's local paper (along with a bottle of water and some vanilla wafers) so I can sift through the classifieds. But I've since set it aside so I can finish some of these assignments.

My body, today, I am free to admit, feels slightly out-of-control, and I can sense - strangely enough - my heart's pulsating beats through my shirt. My arms and legs can't seem to stay still, and while I process today's work they act as an unfortunate diversion. I feel like I need to *move* - a sensation I am not unfamiliar with - and this is without any tea or caffeine this morning. I believe it may be an anxiety attack, but lack the proper medical knowledge to make such a judgment.

Before getting started I find my attention diverted and suddenly fixated on the postcard from France that a lady whose name (I think) is Jan from Human Resources gave me after we had a long chat about the Louvre, which I told her I always wanted to see and she was all too keen to tell me about. The card's color is magenta, and it's made up of many different pictures - a collage, I guess - of buildings, of trees, luscious landscapes and of French citizens walking and chatting with each other on a semi-populated street. All of the images are serene and simple and, when taken collectively, present something remarkable or different - or at least, remarkable and different in the eyes of an American Administrative Technological Assistant who's never been out of the country. I wonder something: on the desks in Paris, or, better yet, in France in general, do they tack up pictures of other countries/islands/resorts? Are these images of Times Square, the Grand Canyon, the Luxor in Vegas, the Fisherman's Wharf in San Francisco (speaking only of America)? Do the French longingly gaze at mesmerizing images like these when they feel downtrodden and ponder on exactly how *fantastic* it would be to do anything but the task at hand?

My thoughts are interrupted by a phone call.

I reluctantly lift up the receiver.

"Yes."

"Hi Devon, it's Mary Nichols from Network Services," the sweet voice answers, "Do you remember in March when you put in a request for a new computer? Well, good news ... the order was finally accepted and the new machine should be installed in about a week. But if you could, try to make sure everything's backed up first."

"How do I do that, exactly?" I ask, staring at the paneled ceiling above and wishing it were a skylight so I could see the clouds.

"Come on down to the second floor and I'll give you some documentation and a disk."

I pause. "Now?"

"Now's fine."

"All right. I'll see you soon. Bye."

"Bye."

I'm astounded, in a way - my voice was heard. I've been pecking away at the abacus in front of me too long and need a change of machinery, and, since I'm not the one who has to cover the expenses, why not?

I take a sip of the bottled water (which could have either been poured from a faucet in Maine or from the tip of the Mendenhall) and proceed to the elevator, through the uninhabited hallways. I push the down arrow and wait for the man-sized scale to find its way to me. When it arrives, it's empty. I push '2.'

Four flights down and a change of equilibrium later, I find myself on the second floor, which is identical to my floor - floor six - but with one difference - the sign on the wall indicates a '2.' After getting my geographical bearing, I proceed left and stroll past several offices filled with boxes and paper and view blocking cream-colored wall-dividers.

When I arrive at my destination I don't bother knocking and slowly creak the door open. There are green and blue and red and yellow binders stacked all on top of each other, along with a myriad of stuffed manila folders ripping at the corners and photocopy machines, in a big long row, all pinching each others' sides. I see a large carton ripped to pieces with white Styrofoam peanuts littered around it. I stop a tall, lanky man with glasses (that look more like aviator goggles and are clearly too large for his head) where Mary is. He points to the right and tells me to follow the blue stripe in the carpet to the conference room. I make my way past a long wall of cubicles and head straight to the vacant, slightly dusty conference room, which smells of brewing hazelnut coffee (although no pot is in sight). A rectangular oak table sits in the center of the room, surrounded by ten unpadded wooden chairs.

At the far end of the long room is Mary's door. I knock on the wall since the door is all the way open and don't just want to step in.

"Come in," the voice says. She is focused on the paperwork covering her desk and doesn't bother to glance upward.

I walk in hesitantly, expending entirely too much mental energy trying to figure out what to say next. "Hi, you called about the disk and...."

"Oh, hello Devon. I have that for you right-," she says as she starts rifling through her oak desk, a shrunken version of the conference table, moves to the steel filing cabinet behind her, then to a large cardboard box labeled "Fragile."

"Someone moved them on me," she says, as she sifts through more piles and piles and stacks of whatever is by her desk. By my feet there are two computer towers lying sideways, on top of each other, with an adding machine set on top of them, its cord tied in a bundle with a rubber band.

"It seems as if you need your own personal assistant to keep this place in line," I tell her, as I examine the side of her face which is caked with foundation and overly pale, which tells me she is probably in her mid-forties and her skin no longer keeps that taut-consistency it possessed years earlier. The suit she's wearing is entirely red, and could hurt your eyes if you stared too long.

Before I make a comment about the poster-type Van Gogh print she has to the right of her oak desk ("Starry Night"), she emerges victorious with the disk and a photocopied 'how-to' pamphlet. "Ta da," she emits as she raises the object in the air. "I knew it was here."

She hands it to me and apologizes for it being lost in the clutter. "Did you say something before? I didn't hear you."

"Well, I said that from the looks of this place it's as if you could use a Personal Assistant to help you straighten things out."

She rolls her eyes. "What do you mean *need*? I have an Assistant. But she's never here, she's always roaming here or there, on the phone. I understand you need time to talk, but there's no ... *prioritizing* with her."

"Where is she now?"

"In the cafeteria. I don't know. I wanted to give her a pager, but she'd just set it someplace and let it buzz."

"Sorry to hear that."

"Oh, I shouldn't say that. You know about office ethics and such. I shouldn't say derogatory things, but, it's, you just get a little sick of doing everything yourself."

"I know what you mean. But letting it out is normal, it's cathartic, I think. You're just releasing tension."

"It's already been a long day. You'd better get going and work on that - if you have any questions, you'd better call me because I can't find anyone else."

"Thanks for everything."

"Sure." She returns to her desk and papers and computer work.

As I walk out of the conference room, the Network Services office, the halls, I keep thinking about whether I came across as nosey or indignant or anything like that or seemed rushed or anything of the sort. I should have also put a good word in for myself regarding the Assistant job in case she eliminates whoever is occupying that spot now but then double over that thought with hesitancies such as whether or not I want to work for that department and what the job entails and how much is dumped on me.

And I should have mentioned the Van Gogh, for the hell of it.

I ride back up the (still) vacant elevator to my floor and promptly return to my seat. I sip at the now-room temperature bottled water, and break open the pack of vanilla wafers I carefully separated into piles according to color out of extreme boredom. I should have prepared a bagged lunch for myself but ran out of lunchmeat.

Instead of processing the two claims in my steel-mesh rack I decide to burrow through the classified ads in the paper, which I've been putting off all afternoon. I realize this job pays sufficiently ($36k and every benefit known to man), and they are giving me a new computer but I feel *wanting*, and need to do something during the day to keep me from thinking about my own thoughts. A lot of the ads require extensive computer training - which I do not possess, knowledge of this programming language or that database software, and without any real desire to pursue a field in things of that nature. My grandmother always told me to be either a (a.) priest or a (b.) plumber. "You'll never be out of a job," she would always advise, God rest her soul.

Here's a quickie sample of one of the positions:

TRACTOR TRAILER DRIVER. Home every night. 1 year driving exp req & 6 mnths dump exp pref'd but will train right individual. NJ, PA, NY, DE. Good pay & benefits.

Note how it says "good" not "great" pay. "Good" is four letters, "great" is five, so it wouldn't have cost them much more to change the wording. While trucking would certainly get me out of an office, my apartment or any other type of enclosed situation, it's always seemed to be a dirty job to me, given the representation of truckers via the media. Plus, I don't have any trucking certification, and have difficulty parallel parking my Honda Civic nonetheless a football-field sized centipede.

Honestly - all of these ads (I'm generalizing - bear with me) require either certification or experience or need this or need that that potentially good people willing to learn are deterred from applying or outright ignore.

There are over fifty job ads in here for sales people needed, but I seriously doubt whether or not I could perform such a job and get paid for lying. In fact, I'd probably hate my job so much that I'd make a game out of deterring people from buying any of the products. "This _____, my good lady/sir/young gent/young miss," I would announce, with crinkled eyebrows, "*this* is garbage. It is not worth your money, as it was made by _____ [insert derogatory term]. Where you *should* go is _____," giving the competition a boost in sales.

[Side note: I've made an interesting observation (well, all right, not exactly interesting to everyone, but interesting to me): when going car shopping with my parents four years ago, I noticed a *significant percentage* of car salespeople are smokers. We went from dealership to dealership, bargaining with this one and that one, and everywhere it was fairly consistent. Sometimes I would sit in the car with a magazine while mother dickered prices with poor, stressed out 40-somethings with thick mustaches, and watch them come out, one at a time, like a revolving door, lighting up, passionately inhaling, exhaling, then doing mini-strolls around the pavement, then tossing the cigarette back into the bushes, only to be replaced by a co-worker who would do the same thing. I didn't actually *write down* any of this, and don't know if it was more women or men or if I'm just pointing out *the obvious*, but I thought it was of slight interest. My interpretation is that salespeople tend to be naturally anxious and impatient and, yes, bored, and cigarettes are simply something to use to pass time.]

My eye catches another ad, in all bold:

CAB DRIVERS needed immediately. Full & part time. Excellent pay. Good driving record req. Apply at Quick Service Taxi...

"Excellent pay." I certainly like that. Quick Service Taxi certainly isn't scotch with the lengthy adjectives. But cabbies are regarded in the same light truck drivers are, and naturally the position isn't glamorous, and you are stuck in a car, and I would have to work nights. But I do have a perfect driving record!

All in all, the majority of these ads disappoint me and I pitch the entire paper in the green recycling waste can. I finish the water, brush the colorful candy bits off the desk and stare at my cheap LCD clock, which stares right back at me.

5.

While preparing tonight's dish of plain Ramen noodles, a butter-flavored microwaveable potato (it's surprisingly low in fat, considering all the "butter"), and a can of Green Giant sweet corn, I decide to call up Davis and see what he's doing tonight - something I rarely do (he normally phones me). I haven't spoken to Davis in about two weeks - he's been in Amarillo, Texas with his now-girlfriend Marie Kelly to visit her relatives down there. He promised me he'd call when he came back, but probably tried to reach me when I wasn't there. I kept thinking he could have left a message on the answering machine I got for Christmas last year, but then realized that the answering machine was shattered on Riverslide Lane about two months ago, courtesy of yours truly. Apparently AT&T doesn't make equipment that can withstand being hurled off the balcony of an apartment some forty-odd feet above the ground. I forgot to lodge a complaint with Sterling (Davis' doppelganger), who did not buy me the phone, but just so happens to be presently employed as a Customer Service Representative at AT&T.

I hear the phone ringing.

A gravelly voice answers. "Huh?"

"It's me. What's going on?"

Davis clears his throat. "He-hey - I forgot to call you, sorry about that."

"What's with your voice?"

"Woke up."

"Now?" I look at the stained yellow circular clock near the stove on the kitchen wall, "It's 5:20 [PM]. What do you mean woke up?"

There's a pause. "I took a day off today. My allergies are bothering me a little."

"Oh."

"Oh what?"

"So I guess nothing's going on tonight, then, right?"

I don't hear anything.

"Davis?"

"I'm trying to put my pants on."

"How sick are you?"

"Sick? No no no, I'm not sick. I could have gone in - just wanted a day off." He clears his throat.

"No, no I mean, if you can't-"

"I can, I can. What are you thinking of?"

"Anything. Well, what ti … um, do you want to call Sterling or should I?" The microwave is beeping - the frozen potato is finished.

"I'll call him after I shower. Did you eat yet?"

"I'm eating now, but not much."

"Okay … I'll go and call you back."

"Talk to you in a bit."

"Yep." He hangs up first.

I go to the microwave to take out the steaming hot bowl, which is all I had to put it in. I make good use of the clean dishtowel to carry the bowl over to the table.

While I've thought about this several times, I fail to come up with a plausible answer as to *why* Davis and Sterling associate with me or return the (few) phone calls I transmit their way or why they take me anyplace, as they could very well find someone better suited for their personalities to accompany them (they do have another travelling companion - Eric - but he's often times busy with work or whatever he says he has to do all day). To put it simply, Davis and Sterling are two creatures from the same cocoon, more like each other than me. I find most of their behavior to be frighteningly erratic, sometimes puerile, and I grow to loathe their presence, yet am strangely interested in them, less as people but more as 'things' to watch. This sounds harsh on my part, but I feel it's the truth.

Now, the true reason as to why I'm calling them is for a bit of advice. No, I'm not averse to asking others what they think I should do - often I become trapped in this mental web I construct and end up more baffled and stressed afterwards than calm and focused. Believe it or not, when they are willing, both Sterling and Davis can - and have - offered decent advice in the past (they suggested which college I should go to, backed me up when I decided to change majors and take up psychology, sided with me when I would end up in arguments with parents, peers, professors, etc), leading me to seek them out again. It sounds selfish, I realize, but it's not as if I have anyone knocking down my door, or a therapist to spout to. Granted, they have to be willing to take up such topics with me - I have noticed, as of late, their patience levels dropping considerably and less willing to discuss potentially weighty issues.

Since the Ramen noodles I'm chewing on aren't high in fat, I hope we go someplace tonight - a restaurant, hopefully - so I can get something more substantial in my stomach (I must run to the store tomorrow to buy vegetables and tea and kiwis and frozen vegetable medleys). I don't really enjoy the restaurant atmosphere as much as I should - too many people, too loud, too many distractions, too much table and seat grime - but Davis is fond of restaurants and coffee and he always thinks he's going to see someone he knows.

Time passes - approx. 45 minutes. The phone rings. It's Davis.

It sounds like someone is blowing into the phone. "I'm calling you from my car phone. We're on our way, but I need gas, so, expect us in-" he says something I can't make out to Sterling, who is with him in the car, "about twenty minutes or so."

"Take your time," I reply, and start on my dishes. I haven't done them in two days out of laziness and take time scrubbing the counters. I use Lemon-scented Palmolive - a heaping amount - in the sink to create more bubbles and thus more detergent and cleaning action for sparkling dishes. I also light up a vanilla cookie scented Yankee Candle in the center of my kitchen table to add aroma.

In regards to Sterling, right now certainly isn't the best time in his life. About eight months ago (I'm guessing here), he and Davis and that Eric fellow were trolling for women and ended up at a party on Glendon Drive seven or eight miles from where I live. I didn't go with them that night - I had a severe cluster headache and had difficulty standing up and was basically lying on the floor, my stomach filled with Mylanta, Tylenol and water, feeling like I was going to bring it all up, and then some. It was Eric who apparently knew about this "gathering," and took them there, and there were a lot of "young, young" females there and who knows exactly what went on, but the conclusion essentially involves Sterling - not the other two - in a lawsuit. Details are shaky - no one mentions it, and when it is brought up, primarily by me, they mostly eye each other and say nothing - and Sterling is hardly the smoothest, most intelligent person I know, nor is he really that funny, but apparently he has a talent for seducing younger, more impressionable girls. Time moves on and I suppose the girl says something to her parents (What teenage girl discusses such things with her elders? Isn't this the era of keeping parents in the dark?) and they're horrified at how old he is and how young she is, and they file charges. I've basically pieced this together from the verbal snippets I collected, and I can't verify my version's accuracy. Personally, that's not the kicker: my mother is his attorney (for the civil charges, someone else I guess took care of the criminal) and not even she would tell me anything, although I continue to prod. Apparently she doesn't trust me, or he doesn't trust me. Or no one does, for some reason.

When I get around to thinking about it, too many questions arise to make sense out of it. A few, off the cuff: Why didn't Davis intervene? Did he know? Where was Eric? Who is this girl? How much is the lawsuit worth? Why isn't he in jail? Is the case dismissed? Is it just starting? Why isn't anyone talking?

I have planned, for sometime now, to get the answers - on my own. I concocted a plan to - in the near future - to break into my mother's office building and find the paper work and details, or at least try to find something on her computer. Call this voyeuristic, call it sick, but I take personal offense when I'm not trusted, especially by people I've known for a long time.

Just as I begin to rearrange scattered newspapers on the floor there's a knock at the door.

I unlock it and give greeting and they make their way in - Davis wearing a thin black raincoat (who knows why), Sterling a red sweater. Both are grossly taller than I am.

"That smells good - what is it?" Davis asks.

"A candle," I reply, slightly impatient. "Where are we going?"

He works his way over to the candle and picks it up, reading the label. "Wow-" he sets the jar back down, "- vanilla cookie. Where'd you get this?"

"The mall."

"I'll have to get one for Marie."

He looks at Sterling, who is leafing through a book I have on insects. He turns back to me. "Now what?"

I shrug, and look at Sterling. "What do you think?"

He puts the book down on the carpet. "We should go get something to eat and figure it out from there."

"I have a couple of ideas, but-" Davis volunteers.

"Like?" I ask.

He shakes his head slightly. "For now, let's just go eat."

We all nod in agreement, and I grab my keys, my sunglasses, a small bottle of Saline eye drops in case my contacts start to antagonize my eyes and a handkerchief. I blow out the candle, glance around to see if there's anything else I'm forgetting (the balcony slide door and the windows are all closed), lock up and proceed downstairs. We pile into Davis's Camaro, which possesses a flashy red glimmer to it, and set off. The car is literally stockpiled with every piece of advanced audio equipment available, but doesn't have what I would want if buying something like this - a sunroof. But Davis tells me that he knows of a guy who had a sunroof in his Ford and it just kept leaking.

The car's sound system is churning out some jumpy dance song with a seemingly endless bouncy drum loop, and I can feel the seat cushion behind me vibrating against my head, which is admittedly uncomfortable and deafening (I'm in the backseat, as always). There isn't a lot of traffic out tonight and the sky is clear and I take both to be good signs and hope the restaurant we go to isn't that crowded, or that we don't have an exaggeratingly long wait.

"Hey-" I shout, as I lean forward and try to make myself heard over the wind blowing from the lowered windows as well as the synthesizers and keyboards. "Which restaurant are we going to?"

Sterling turns his head. "Davis knows of this new place up by the Newport Inn. Some guy at work told him it has great steaks and stuff like that and he wanted to try it. That good?"

"Yeah," is all I say, although I admit I'm a tad peeved - they didn't ask me where I wanted to go. But I don't feel like throwing a snit - I did call them after all - so I simply sit back. There's a new copy of some men-only fashion-sports-dating magazine on the seat that I browse through. I take interest in the section on the different types of martinis when Davis shouts back to me.

"I almost forgot to tell you. When I was on vacation and Marie and I spent some time going through those junk shops they have all over the place, I was in this novelty store and I was looking at bumper stickers and saw this one-" he nudges to Sterling and points to the floor "-and thought I had to buy this for you. Marie thought it was funny." He says something to Sterling again and motions to the floor, and Sterling leans over and grabs a thin brown bag and hands it to me.

I open the bag and take out the only item inside. The sticker reads (with a blue background and tiny white lettering):

Clean living makes for good health

... which he tells me has something to do with a joke I apparently made a few months ago but I can't recall and both of them laugh about. They try to remind me of what it was about, but I'm still loose on details. Regrettably, they drop it, and I probe my memory. Nothing comes up.

Not much else is said on the drive between any of us - they're to busy trying to show off the car to girls in black Volkswagens driving alongside us on the highway, but I ignore any such bravado. In the past I would have said something to them about leaving people alone - like when they would drive past people years ago and try to throw bits of trash into their open windows during the summer, or bring a camera along and take pictures of the other drivers' faces just to unnerve them.

The restaurant, "Alexander's" is a deceptive meat-and-potatoes-and-alcohol-kind-of-place but with a limited menu and high-priced items. Their steak dinners look good, but they run in the $15-$18 range - I hope I brought enough money. We are notably underdressed compared to those who have on suit jackets, but there are a few stragglers - like us - wandering about with shorts and T-shirts on, getting soup from the vast salad bar.

Inside "Alexander's" are a lot of plants in the long waiting room where we sit huddled on tiny benches while slowly growing impatient. We aren't the only ones, as a middle-aged couple standing nearby mumble to each other as to whether or not they should leave. They make their way over to the brunette woman at the wood podium - who could hardly give half-a-damn as to whether or not you made reservations - and restrain themselves and inquire as to what-is-going-on-because-we-called-ahead-of-time but she will have nothing to do with them and nods sarcastically and chants management-constructed koans like, "We're here to serve you" and "Please be patient, you're next on the list" or "Try a drink from the bar," but they are still not satisfied and back away from the podium slowly.

Davis mentions something about kicking the woman to death but I ignore him.

When we do get seated - some hour and a half later - none of us are in a fit mood to speak or be spoken to. The restaurant is partitioned into a multitude of sections, each one thoroughly packed with people, noisy and smelling of grilled food. The section we're placed in reminds me of a cottage, with wood paneling all around and rustic wood beams stretched across the high ceiling. A large painting of mostly green and white and blue brushstrokes conceals most of the northern-most wall. A smaller painting behind me is of a Victorian-age woman in a white dress that looks more like a garbage bag than suitable attire, holding a lilac in her right hand. Behind her: a castle.

Apparently Davis and Sterling don't mind the smoking or excessive noise coming from everywhere, and are too focused on examining the menu for them to care much about anything.

Davis keeps going back from the second page to the first, then back to the second, then to the first. "Is this it?" He asks.

"I guess so." I tell him.

Sterling turns to me, "Did you bring enough money?"

"I brought twenty," I say. "I think that will be enough."

"Christ this place is fucking expensive."

Davis defends himself. "Chris never mentioned the prices."

"Or the long wait," Sterling retorts.

Our waiter - a thin, chiseled man with a 5 o'clock shadow and a receding hairline asks for our drink order. For all of us, it's usually the same: two Miller Genuine Drafts and a glass of water. If you guessed the water is mine, you are correct. Shockingly, I never get hell for it - they never argue with me as to what I should or should not drink. I guess I trained them after all these years to overlook my eccentricities (or, perhaps, ignore them). No matter.

After he leaves I try to break into Serious Conversation Mode, but I have the feeling the long wait has basically ruined everyone's mood. Sterling continuously plays with his Timex watch, twisting the band around his wrist, while Davis scans the room thoroughly. Sterling asks us what today's date is but none of us knows for sure.

"I think it's the 16th," Davis blurts, "but I may be mistaken."

Sterling tinkers with the watch's buttons.

I lunge.

"Listen - the reason I called both of you was because, well, I need some advice and I wanted to run my idea past you before I did anything, just because, well, it's - I didn't want to just jump and-"

"About what?" Davis interrupts.

"My job. I'm, I think I've been there too long. I feel, I've been looking through the paper-"

Davis interrupts again. "What? Leave?" He shakes his head, adjusts his collar. "Didn't you tell me it was easy? You're probably making more than him-" he points to Sterling. "You know what I did today? I soldered wires onto a circuit board, had a two hour lunch, talked to Dave for a while, left, and that was it. It's dull, but I'm making too much to skip out for something lower."

"But you earn almost twice what I make."

"You're not an engineer. Go back and get an engineering degree."

Sterling steps in. "I'm not sure Dev here's school material."

"Not anymore," Davis says.

"What were you thinking of?" Sterling asks.

"I don't know. Maybe a truck driver or taxi driver."

Both laugh. "Your folks will be real pleased with their offspring driving a truck," Davis chokes out, after sipping down some of his beverage. Apparently neither remembers that I did, at one time, work as a janitor.

Sterling volunteers his help by offering to talk to Human Resources at AT&T. "They're hiring in the customer service end where I'm at."

I shrug. "Thanks, but it's a long drive, and I don't know much about computers."

"They could teach you what you need to know. But you've got to show up on time - you punch a clock. None of that twenty-five minutes late shit you pull over there will work. I was four minutes late the other day and the Floor Leader told me about it. I mean, it was four minutes."

A side point that isn't really relevant: Sterling, in the past, was prone to massive flights of imaginative verbosity, in which he takes simple stories and 'novelizes' them. In junior high, he had a vacation photo that he took with his Dad's Pentax K1000 of a river (the Colorado?). After developing the film he noticed that in the pristine sky there was this silver object surrounded by a reddish haze. He was convinced that this shiny, airborne particle was a UFO. He brought the picture to class one day and concocted all sorts of stories about the time and place when the image was taken, and about a "WHOOSHING" noise he heard that day, but no one - not Davis, nor myself - believed him. Potential theories: (a.) bad film, (b.) bad camera, (c.) reflection of sunlight or (d.) a bloody bird, (e.) an airplane's reflection. As a prank, John Tissler put a cassette recorder with the Orson Welles rendition of "War of the Worlds" inside his locker before school and pressed play. Sterling found it, when he arrived, in a hallway filled with laughing students and teachers, who thought it was charming and were simply teasing him. He had a good sense of humor about it at the time, but found John's car after school one day and smashed all of his windows. Suspension naturally followed. He hasn't discussed matters pertaining to the supernatural openly since that day. (Summary: when he says "four minutes" it was probably "forty").

"Four minutes?" I goad. "It *had* to have been longer."

"No," he insists. "My car clock is the same as the clock inside..." etc., etc. and on and on.

I interrupt. "Did I mention they're getting me a new computer?"

"See?" Davis stresses. "Just read your damn paper or color or drink coffee. Hell, in a few months you could try for a raise. Just keep making money and getting away with everything."

Sterling nods in mindless agreement, although I'd expect nothing less.

"But I just feel like I'm a damned stereotype. You know," I say.

Davis just looks at me with puzzlement. "I'm not going to ask what you mean."

The waiter arrives, and we order: two steak dinners and a bowl of Manhattan clam chowder for me.

Not satisfied with the lack of empathy on their side I alter my focus from the table and shift it to the other patrons inhabiting the same space as I, yet engaging in their own private conversations, trying to solve their own private dilemmas, arguing over a film or book or moot point, gossiping with perverted curiosity. My attention is directed to a chubby man in a suit in the corner of the room, who sits alone with a cigarette dangling from his mouth (I thought we were in non-smoking), arms folded, elbows rested on the table. The lower right hand corner of the rectangular abstract painting appears to poke him right in the head. He's looking at a twenty-something teenage girl at a table ten feet away from him, facing him, but she doesn't appear to notice (or, if she does notice, she is quite deft at concealing her irritation and discomfort). The girl is laughing with her two female friends across from her who have their backs to the man - they're all drinking daiquiris and fidgeting and bouncing their lower legs about under the table and telling stories and occupying their own self-contained worlds. I think the man would do anything just to sit at their table, maybe talk, maybe not, but just sit there and smoke his cigarette. But he's not, and his only companion is the Gibson Martini sitting in front of him (it is certainly not his first).

Davis catches on to my sudden, prolonged silence and attempts to lure me back.

"Where do you want to head to tonight? Ideas?"

I'm indifferent. "Don't care."

Sterling chimes in: "How about a movie?"

Davis examines his watch. "I think we've missed everything by the time we leave here."

Sterling thinks a bit. "Didn't you say you had an idea before?"

"Yeah, we could do that." Sterling nods.

"What idea?" I ask. No one answers.

The waiter arrives sometime later with our meals, which we eat in silence, after the mindless bickering has subsided and we arrive at a stalemate (or at least I did). While sipping the scalding hot clam chowder (which is a little too flat), I continue watching the Single Guy and The Giggling Girls Saga, which is already under way. I'm guessing the man is working on his fourth martini, as the third was half-finished last I turned away, and this one is full (it could, very well, be the fifth). The girls are busy flirting with their gawky waiter who is not handsome but a male nonetheless. The girls are free to engage in this pseudo chatter/come-on session with the waiter because of safety in numbers - there are three of them and one of him.

Sterling and Davis finish up their food in silence, we get the check, pay for our respective meals (mine being $7), leave a tip and make our way out. Before walking out of this section of the restaurant I take one last glance back at the man, working hard on his pack of cigarettes. I would love to see the conclusion, and if he takes the plunge or comes to his senses, and who leaves first, but I don't and the whole thing feels rather anti-climactic.

In the car I come to and ask where we're headed.

"If you'd been paying attention you'd have heard we were going to a party Eric told us about," Davis informs me.

I lean forward so the two in the front can hear me over the dance-trance-house music that won't leave me alone. "Are you sure that's a good idea? I mean - considering what happened with Sterling at a 'party' that one time."

Sterling is quick to dart his head around at me. "If you want to go home, we'll drop you off."

"Where's this thing at?" I inquire.

"Don't worry about it," a voice says - I think it's Davis.

So I sit back and gaze up at the night sky. I - for some reason - have always loved the dark and the night. I did when I was younger, too. I think better at night and feel better at night. For me, it's the absence of people talking, of cars, of dogs snarling, of TVs churning, computers humming, beeping, machines screeching and banging. At night there has always been this - calm - that comes over me. In college I would often only go out at 1 AM or 2 AM on a weekday (not weekend) and just stroll around, taking in the smell of the breeze, finding comfort in the lack of stress, the serenity. In the wintertime I made sure to head out all bundled up when it was snowing at night, and relish the cold, numb feeling in my eyes, the burning sensation in my cheeks, the way street lamps and the moon collaborated, providing enough lighting to see the simple, elegant, perfectly constructed flakes fall effortlessly from the sky, in an endless barrage. I recall writing in my journal how I felt this Wintertime Night Walk was an almost-mystical experience for me, although that sounds a bit silly. Either way, it would be memories of those walks that would comprise my memory of those four years, and not much else.

In going tonight with these two I had a goal, of sorts, to converse, to discuss, because I don't have anyone else to talk with, and wanted verification that it was okay to move on, that yeah, you should challenge yourself, that trying new things is acceptable, at least once in a while.

The Camaro purrs along, darting from lane to lane, leaping from vacant space to vacant space, shifting, sliding. Davis is usually the chauffeur for the two of us, and neither of us complains - Sterling likes riding in the shiny, sporty car, I just hate driving.

When we arrive, it's in a long parking lot, half-filled with cars of all sorts and only a single streetlight to illuminate the yards of asphalt. I look around and don't see any other streetlights anywhere near here, or perhaps it is the vacant, dirty buildings that block their glow.

The two are discussing some concert Eric said he went to and got elbowed in the ribs and I interrupt, posing a question: "Is Eric here?"

"I don't know. I think so," Davis answers.

We go down the sidewalk a bit until we encounter a mob of strange derelicts and teenagers and riff raff surrounding the entrance to a wide, expansive warehouse - or what I take to be a warehouse - which is surrounded on all sides by other, taller buildings, most of which have boards over the windows and graffiti on the walls. The music - the noise - coming from inside the dance laboratory is going thuuummppp-whuuummppp-thuuummppp and I'm surprised the cops aren't here to straighten shit out. But from the looks of the area we're in, with no lighting and dingy, crumbling buildings (which I only half make out), it is hardly what one would consider a residential area and I'm assuming no one honestly cares. While I'm scanning the territory I'm trying to figure out what town we're in, what street we're on, but I get a tug on my button-down blue-and-white checkered shirt by Davis and he motions to go in.

"Do we have to pay?" I ask, naively.

"Nope, private thing," he tells me.

In order to enter we tiptoe past the denizens surrounding the entrance, all in a little huddle. I say *denizens* but they don't look as radical as you might think - there are guys wearing T-shirts and girls with tank-tops, normal hair-cuts and plastic cups attached to their hands, brimming with murky spirits. I get a good look at some of the shirts, and the one I like most is the one that says:

MUST BE
THIS TALL
TO RIDE ME

... which is actually *not* the funniest part. The funny part is the Ronald McDonald-esque clown in the lower right-hand corner of the shirt with his arm extended and 4'1" written by the hand.

As we head inside, our retinas are given a Christmas gift in the form of 20,000 some-odd watts of high-energy strobe lights beaming from every direction. I immediately flinch and turn my head, startled. Following Sterling I notice there is a metal staircase leading down a frigid, narrow hallway. Slowly growing accustomed to this visual disturbance I get more of a bearing as to what type of place this is inside. The walls are mostly brick - from what I can tell - and there are large stone pillars running from floor to ceiling, cylindrical in shape. It's quite cool down here, and an unwelcome draft takes hold of my exposed skin. The smell - how to describe it - it's a combination of mold, mildew and human sweat, and quite strong at that, considering the vast size of the warehouse, now devoid of crates, workers and machinery and replaced with dancing, impulsive individuals. I'm overwhelmed by how many people there are, talking, gyrating, shaking, and I'm mesmerized by the way the movements of those dancing seem jerky and slow because of the strobe effects - it's the equivalent of taking every other frame out of a film and replacing those frames with ones of a solid color.

I get carried away examining the area and trying to take in the place objectively and in the meantime lose the two people I came in with. Since I don't intend to dance, can't dance, feel too old to dance, can't hear too well or see too well, and feel uncomfortable just standing still, I decide to make the rounds. As I make my way over to the left wall I realize that there are windows in there, but they are tiny and about twenty-five feet above the ground. I can't tell whether or not you can open them or what purpose they serve (I'm guessing they're either for decoration or for looking in, not out), but wish they were all open to dissipate the stagnant, translucent fog surrounding me.

It's hard to tell exactly what went on in this place before it shut down, although there is certainly evidence all around me. For starters, there's a lot of leftover equipment like forklifts and dirty little four-wheel delivery trucks pinned in the corners and roped off from the public. My grandmother used to work in a candy factory for about forty-five years - an ungodly number, I realize - and when she showed it to me when I was little I was startled by the dusty dank expansiveness of it, how large the shipping warehouse looked filled with pallets stacked half-way to the roof with fluff and marshmallow and jelly beans and how such sweet goodness trapped inside cardboard boxes could stay for so long in such murky filth before being taken away by trucks.

I continue making my rounds, wandering around in perfect circles. Most people dancing don't seem to notice me, and I think this is a good thing. I spot some vendor tables, set up and covered with cardboard signs, some selling music from local bands, some selling T-shirts and one in particular handing out brochures about some "Save the _____" Foundation (with the 'blank' being an animal, vegetable or mineral).

My goal to find Davis and Sterling - or just one of them - is futile as there are hundreds and hundreds of people crammed in this loud, semi-lucid box and I'm not the tallest person here to see over them. At this point I'm desperately growing bored and honestly want to leave - I'm thirsty from the Manhattan Clam Chowder I ate a while ago, but don't see anything around that looks like clean water.

Too much time passes and I'm sick of roaming around, as if I were on a monitored exercise program at the local prison, forced to pace around the courtyard. I'm sick of saying, "Excuse me" and "I'm sorry" to every person I bump into (whether it's my fault or not) and I'm sick of the accompanying dirty looks (as if I *intentionally* run into people for kicks). I decide to find a wall - away from any booth, table or sound speaker to lean against and stay out of everybody's way.

The area I end up at is near the steel steps leading up and out. I figure that if I don't see either Davis or Sterling in the next couple of minutes I'm just going to bolt upstairs and let them try to find me. The combination of lights and my own claustrophobia are bothering me - I can't do anything about the claustrophobia, but I do take out my sunglasses from my shirt pocket and put them on to try to save my eyes for a little bit. They mute the brightness of the flashes but also make everyone else formerly hard to see now almost impossible to make out. I find bright lights to be intensely annoying.

Without drugs of any sort I begin to fall under the trance of the room and slouch against the brick wall that's behind me. I rest my head uncomfortably against the gritty surface, and gaze up at the rectangular ceiling filled with lights of all sorts, operating in different patterns. X minutes pass and I get startled by someone's voice near me, and I become alert and work my way to my feet.

"You look so bored and purposely aloof!" the voice tells me. It's high pitched and loud and very feminine. The owner of the voice is standing dangerously close to me, violating my 'red zone' or personal space. I slowly edge away as I reply.

"I'm just really tired." I say, looking at her. She's alone right now, like me, but I'm guessing her friends are elsewhere drinking something or dancing in a different area. Her face has a distinguished angular shape to it, and she isn't wearing anything overly freakish, just shorts and a tank top. Her bare flesh and hair are coated with sparkling glitter. She has a little bit of green face paint on her cheeks.

"Tired? Did you dance too much?"

"No. I'm actually waiting for two people. They're here, somewhere." I motion to the mass of humanity in the center of the room.

"Ah," she says. "I was just thinking you look like...." and I can't make out the rest of what she says.

"What?"

"Why don't you try dancing a little?"

"I don't know how."

"Neither does anybody else. All you have to do is jump around. It's that easy. No one gives a fuck. It's not a contest."

"You go ahead. Thank you." I'm staring, mesmerized, at the DJ behind the platform and his enormous headphones.

Then she does the unthinkable - she takes the sunglasses off my face. I immediately reach up but she's too quick and the right stem pokes me in the eye. "No no no no," she keeps saying, playfully, and skips away. If they were the cheap pair I bought at a thrift shop I'd let her take them, but these are my favorite, most expensive pair and I've grown attached. I leap towards her, and grab her right arm, which is sweaty and thin.

"Look, I'm sorry-" I say, rubbing my right eye with my left hand. "-I'm just out of my element here. "

She just looks at me. "What's wrong with you?"

I'm not sure what she means. I offer something: "The sunglasses help me from having a seizure."

Her eyebrows raise and come together. "Don't you like me?"

I'm taken back. "It's not that, I - I, you look, you look fine, and you seem nice, I'm just, umm ... lost."

"About what?"

It's now that I notice that her eyes are unusually shaky and unfixed, almost like the ball inside of a spherical compass, moving about slightly as if trying to look at everything at once. It isn't exaggerated, but I can tell.

"What's wrong with *your* eyes?" I ask, curious.

"Nothing. They sting a little."

I tell her to keep the sunglasses and wear them. She asks why. I tell her I feel like I'm her Father or Older Brother and that I want to help the stinging just a little. I actually give in to my thoughts and consider running my fingers through her hair and over her glistening face. She doesn't ask questions, puts the cheap sunglasses on and walks away from me.

———

Time passes and I find myself checking my watch more and more. It's 2-something - I've been here about three hours. I get tired of looking at nothing and ascend the steps for fresh air - something I should have done a long time ago, and avoid the dancing, the thieving sprite and also save my eyes and ears some wear-and-tear. I was scared to before - for some unknown reason - but now I can hardly care - and clank up the steps and out the metal doors that are sticky from something that smells like orange juice.

As soon as I reach the outside and its nocturnal noises, hushed but present, I head for Davis's Camaro, as the realization hits me - and I panic - that they may have left without me (they never, ever, ever have in the past, so this was never an issue previously). I pass a bent "Street Watch" sign that I laugh at, stumble over an empty can of Milwaukee's Best and step over miscellaneous garbage strewn about, potentially from parties past. It's foggy out now, and still hard to see well. I do find the lot, though, and this time it's completely packed full of cars. I find Davis's Camaro, but neither him nor Sterling are inside or anywhere around. The other vehicles range from a multitude of Volkswagons, Fords, Chevrolets to a dinged up Volvo with a bumper sticker on it regarding Tibet and a BMW with an "Amherst College" sticker adorning the back window. Some of the insides of these cars are completely unblemished, while some have magazines and tapes littered all over the place, some have old food containers in plastic bags, and one in particular has a woman's garter hanging from the rear-view mirror.

Since no one is around I sit down alongside the Camaro with my legs spread out along the gravel.

In a half-hour the hooligans surface and make their way towards me. Sterling is staggering a bit, his legs going in a slightly different direction than his torso. Davis acts as a human crutch when needed, keeping Sterling from bumping into him.

Davis is the first to speak. "What the hell are you doing here? We've been roaming around looking for you for half-an-hour. We asked some people if they saw you - we described you - but no one did. It took Jack London over here to figure out you were outside." Sterling is leaning against the car, his hand acting as a visor over his eyes.

"But you two disappeared on me," I say.

"Yeah, but we told you not to leave there."

"I didn't hear you."

Davis gives me a slight nudge with his foot so I can get up and he can open the door.

"You will not believe who was in there."

I get in the car. "Who?"

"Catherine."

I pause. "No."

"I swear. Sterling thought he saw her twice, but couldn't be sure."

"Did he say anything to her?"

"No, he thought maybe he was wrong."

"Did *you* see her?"

"No." He gets in the driver's seat.

"Did you see Eric?"

"No."

"Wasn't he supposed to be here?"

"Who the hell knows with him?"

He looks to see where to put the key to start the car, and there isn't much light around to help.

"You look a little out of it," I notice. "Are you sure you don't want me to drive?"

"Yes." There's a pause. "Wait, no, I got it, I'm fine. Anyway, you don't know how to get us out of here."

"That's because you never told me where here is."

There's a pause. He looks at me in his rearview mirror with a look of puzzlement, then promptly starts the car.

The drive back home is a breeze, for the most part, because the roads and highways are vacant. I try to keep my eyes shut because they burn and I don't have a mirror in front of me to put saline drops in. Sterling, eerily silent, is doubled over in the passenger seat. Davis unwisely keeps one eye on the road, the other on him, making sure he doesn't "puke on the floor mats."

When I do eventually get home - in another hour - safe, but with an awful ringing in my ears, and a sticky feeling over my skin, and the collective scent of both cigarette smoke and grilled food stuck to my clothes and hair, I dart straight to the shower, pulling off everything in my kitchen and tossing it in a Hefty Cinch Sack, which I will most likely dispose of later. Naked and barefooted I skip into the shower on the balls of my feet, turn the water temperature knob on hot and wash four-plus hours off myself.

It's in the shower that I notice that my right hand is covered with glitter - most likely from when I grabbed that girl's arm. There's also glitter on my legs for some reason, and I take extra time to scrub these areas, with Country Apple Shower Wash (complete with exfoliating beads).

I take a silent vow to completely avoid associating with those two for a variety of reasons. I'm not mad at them, it's just that I feel we're all growing, or rather, changing into different people - me different from them, particularly - and not interested in the things they're interested in. We used -

if I recall correctly - to have more *purposeful* conversations, reveal personal issues and problems with each other earlier on in our relationship, and perhaps we've reached the point where - like married couples - we don't really want to hear what each other has to say anymore. Or, in particular, they don't want to hear what I have to say. I can only hope this doesn't sound conceited or anything like that, as I hold no real animosity or loathing towards them (or, perhaps I do and am simply unaware).

When I step out of the shower and under the florescent bathroom lighting I notice the whites of my eyes have turned purple.

6.

Saturdays are always the slowest - but best - days. Both Davis and Sterling spend their Saturdays with either girlfriends or family, and since I don't possess the former or care to deal with the latter I spend the day alone, sorting through journal entries or listening to a sporting event on the radio or dusting the few pieces of furniture I do own or vacuum or doodle on sketch paper.

Last night I got to bed around 4-something and slept until noon when the sound of slamming car doors and general get-going outside stirred me. I awoke, did the usual morning routine of tea and cereal while tuning in to 94.7 (WODE) for the weather report. But before I could pour the water into my Route 66 mug there's a knock on the door. Frightened it could be an unwanted, I tiptoe to the door and glance out the peephole. It's Seth, my neighbor downstairs, with his cat, Capo, tucked under his right arm.

I unlock and open the door. "Good morning."

"No, good afternoon. How's it going?"

"Fine. You need me to take care of the cat, right? How long?"

He laughs. "You're on to me already! I'm going to be away about two weeks. If anyone comes asking for me, tell them I've gone to Santa Fe to hike or take a message. Here's twenty for cat food. Was that enough last time?"

He hands me the money. "Sure, sure."

"If it's any more, let me know."

"I will."

"And here's CapoBall." He hands me the cat's favorite toy, a green rubber ball.

I reluctantly take it. "Have a nice time."

"Sure. And get some rest will you? Your eyes are red." He sets the cat on the floor and it bolts into my apartment, slightly panicking me for a second.

"Will do." And down the steps he goes.

As soon as I close the door I try to hunt down Capo, who is gray/white/black in color, medium-sized, clawed and frantic - it *rubs against* everything: my mattress, my furniture, my clothes, my carpet, and that very *rubbing* makes me shudder. I had a chair a while back with a cloth-type backing to it and I found him one day dangling from the side, razors dug in deep, refusing to let go. Its sheer *zest* is an annoyance - he isn't the stereotypical 'sleepy, moody' cat you always read about. To combat him, I have devised my own method of home protection.

It's called "The House of Good King Capo" - that's what I scribbled on it - and it's of my own personal design. Seth has never provided me with a holding cage or "cat carrier" or one of those little devices used to keep your pet in, and simply lets Capo dart around his apartment. I think it's stupid of him to assume others would just let him do the same. So what I have done in the past and will continue to do is take an empty cardboard box with flaps (I have several), poke many holes in the sides to ensure air flow and take him and his slimy, gnawed play-toy and place them ever-so-gently in the box and duct tape the top shut. Naturally, he flips out, scratching this and that, making loud hissing noises, urinating and defecating all over the base of the box, but I honestly don't care, as I then take the box, filled with cat and ball, and put them on the outside patio. If the box becomes too soiled and soggy I replace it with a clean one. Capo goes through about a box a week.

It's not that I don't feed him, though - I do. I usually stock up on expensive tuna fish or kitty chow at the store and feed Capo twice a day, and put a bowl of skim milk there for him to lap at. When I take him out, though, it usually requires me to put on swimming goggles (I don't swim, I don't know why I have them, but they're here), long rubber gloves and (sometimes) a ski mask to avoid facial lacerations. I do so every time I need to put something in or take something out of the box. I also do it whenever I need to wash him (it's always a struggle when he's in the shower). Seth never complains when I return the cat even though it's super rambunctious and hard to control (he chalks it up to standard-Capo behavior, like "Oh, he's always antsy," etc). He thanks me for taking care of him and usually gives me a few bucks for my efforts. After he leaves I hold my breath and dispose of the last box.

You might wonder why I bother. Well, I see it as neighborly obligation. Amy can't do it - she's highly allergic to animals and pollen and cars and Christ knows what else - and Seth disapproves of how the animals are treated in the shelter (cause for chuckle, I'm sure). My goal is not to harm the feline, only to keep it from clawing my things to pieces, and being a distraction.

The same rules apply again this time around - I confiscate the cat with gloves and goggles, take him to his resting place, toss in the ball, tape up the box, take it outside on the balcony, let it there.

While I sip on the decaffeinated tea and slowly spoon down my Raisin Bran and diced banana, I glance over to the corner of my kitchen (some two feet away) and contemplate as to what I should do with the clothes from last night that are in their own little sack on the floor across from the kitchen table. I figure I could either (a.) throw the clothes away or (b.) wash them and give them to the Salvation Army or (c.) wash them and keep them. I doubt if there are any lasting stains on the clothes, and I don't think the large doses of glitter will ruin them (I'm assuming there is glitter on them), and hope the wash purges them of the myriad of mirror-like colored dots.

The rest of the day I mull over Sterling's supposed observation last night/this morning regarding Catherine, who Davis hasn't mentioned in forever and whom none of us has seen for six or so years.

"The History of Catherine" is a long one. All of us started in grade school together, progressed to high school and essentially grew up with each other. Here's the kit-n-caboodle: Davis and her didn't start going out until sophomore year in high school, and though they had their fights and arguments (mostly over Davis' constant lateness and general lack of empathy) they stayed together until the end of high school, when she left to go to school out in Kentucky or someplace far off and I presume they tried to keep the long-distance relationship going but it eventually fizzled out and they stopped making calls to each other and her family moved to Florida of all places and she (I think) met someone else at school. I tried to console Davis in my usual way of explaining how "people grow apart" or some nonsense I read in a romance novel but he dismissed my advice and attempted to show sympathy as useless psycho prattle. He did, apparently, get over it when he developed a crush on a female electrical engineer at his school, and Catherine hasn't been mentioned much since. In retrospect, I thought she was half-decent towards me, and I was half-decent towards her. The story is old.

As for whether or not 'they' saw her, I'm truly skeptical, and truthfully don't care too much. She hasn't been in the area (that any of the three of us know of) for the last six or seven years - why would she come back now? I know I would not come back if I were away.

7.

Sunday I break down and call Mom to get job advice, which I swore not to but tore my hair out Saturday trying to cautiously *map out* my future, meticulous Step by meticulous Step, and can't decide what to do with myself, my time. I'm not saying she's all-wise or anything of the sort, but she's all I have left, as one of my human forms of therapy. I also wanted to smack myself for making such a gigantic project out of this whole thing - why don't I just close my eyes, wave a finger over the want ads, and where it stops, call/fax/send resume.

The following will be in transcript form (to ensure free-flowing give-and-take, a la Hollywood, a la stenographer-typed courtroom documents), with "Mom" being Mom and "Me" being Me. I'm sorry. That's pretty self-explanatory. I hope you don't mind.

Time: 2:04 PM. The phone rings four times. On the fifth, the receiver is picked up.

Mom: Hello?

Me: What's happening?

Mom: Oh, hi! Not too much. How about with you?

Me: I've been really busy. Say, I need to talk to you about something important, or at least I think it's important.

Mom: Right. Can you hold on a second?

Me: Don't put Dad on.

Mom: He's not here; I have to.... (*she breaks off*)

Me: Hello? Nothing.

I hear clattering in the background, then something that sounds like a loud "thud," then "shit," accompanied by another "thud" and then a faucet running.

Four minutes elapse.

Me: Hello?

Mom: Okay, I'm back.

Mom: I dropped the bowl of strawberries that someone didn't put the lid on tight to and they spilled all over the floor.

Me: Oh.

Mom: What did you want?

Me: Are you in a good mood?

Mom: Oh no.

Me: No, it's nothing *bad*. It's I need to ask you about work-

Mom: Were you fired?

Me: No, I'm just really-

Mom: Are you being bothered by anyone?

Me: No, no, I'm not, it's not that.

Mom: Hmm?

Me: I'm, I want to work someplace else.

Mom: Why? It's not so bad there, is it?

Me: It's not interesting.

Mom: What is?

Me: *Your* job is interesting.

Mom: No it's not. You know it's not.

Me: You get paid more.

Mom: Yeah, but I went more years to - how many times do we need to go over this?

Me: I'm bored.

Mom: At work.

Me: Yeah.

Mom: You sound like a child.

Me: I know.

Mom: You call me to tell me you're bored at work. Join the millions.

Me: I just wanted to try someplace else, try something new.

Mom: You're making good money.

Me: Can't I find another job that gives me around the same?

Mom: Sure, go look.

Me: What do you suggest?

Mom: Look in the paper.

Me: I did.

Mom: Well then what do you want from me?

Me: Maybe I can work for you.

Mom: You know how that would turn out.

Me: Right.

Pause.

Mom: If you are so bored, take a book. Do your drawing or whatever you do. It's the best you can do for now. Aren't there, oh, promotions coming up or anything like that? Do they post?

Me: I don't know.

Mom: What?

Me: Nothing's posted.

Mom: Can't you talk to anyone?

Pause.

Me: (*Lying*) Yeah.

Pause.

Me: (*Changing subject*) Out of curiosity, I was kind of wondering what was going on with Sterling in his-

Mom: For the last time, no.

Me: You're being stubborn.

Mom: What did he tell you?

Me: He didn't say anything.

Mom: He told me not to tell you anything about it, I said I wouldn't.

Me: But I've known him-

Mom: Right, but he's embarrassed and I can't blame him. He doesn't want anyone to know.

Me: Wasn't it in the paper?
Mom: You know what I'm talking about.
Me: Who am I going to tell?
Mom: If he wanted you to know-
Me: Right, just, just forget I said it.
Pause.
Mom: Is that all?
Me: Thanks for everything.
Mom: (*Sighs*) What do you want me to tell you?
Me: Just do me a favor and tell me if you hear anything new, any new positions.
Mom: How would I hear anything?
Me: You know lots of people.
Mom: Not *really.*
Me: Oh come on.
Mom: (*Pause*) All right, but I can't guarantee anything.
Me: I know.
Pause.
Me: I have to go.
Mom: Talk to people at work.
Me: I will. Bye.
Mom: Bye.
Click. Time: 2:12 PM.

What did I expect? Edgy and itching to do something - now - I decide to grab Seth's bicycle in the storage closet and ride to the nearest FastStop for some Tylenol (I seem to have run low) and today's edition of the newspaper, which always has more job listings than any other day of the week. The bike, as I open up the door, is dusty but virtually unscathed - a trinket without much mileage. Frankly, I can't tell if he's ever used it.

The completely black Cannondale is ultra-light as well, which, I figure, suggests that's it's well-crafted and worthy of its price tag. I normally don't venture out on the weekend - especially in the summer - because of all the congestion and people driving and darting and dashing from location to location, matter flowing from space to space, slicing apart the invisible air. I had contemplated driving, but figured that I drove all week and genuinely dislike driving when it's not completely necessary.

Taking $6.00 in cash from the oak dresser with cabinets (instead of drawers) and the bike, I head out of the apartment, walking the bike down three flights of stairs. On the first floor, Amy's apartment is dark and I don't hear noise coming from her television, which is good, because I'm not sure if she would tell Seth I was using his bike, or if he would be pleased with my doing so.

Once outside, I notice some traffic, old people walking and youthful children with toy dump trucks on the curb, unaware of anything around them. Across the street in the other apartment complexes, I see people sitting on their respective balconies, acquiring 'color' from the bright rays. On the balcony of one of these apartments, two young girls are spitting over the edge of the railing, trying to see who can hit the green recycling can on the curb below. When the one nails it, she giggles frantically, and that forces the other one, next to her, to try harder (and spit faster) to match her foe.

I haven't been on a bicycle for quite a number of years, so at first I feel clumsy and awkward. For starters, Seth is taller than I am, which means the seat-setup is custom set for him. However, not exactly mechanically inclined, I decide to simply sit uncomfortably, fearing that any alteration I make will be immediately noticed. After a few minutes of establishing stability, braking and such (as well as making short, gawky U-turns on the narrow pavement for practice), head out to the FastStop.

As I come to notice quickly, the sidewalk is jarringly uneven, with the different cement squares knocked off kilter, as if the San Andreas Fault ran right under the street and on the East Coast. While the bike is well equipped with shock-type devices to adjust to bumpy terrain, the plastic-but-covered-with-a-thin-film-of-fabric bike seat is wrecking havoc on my entire lower area. In the meantime, I have to craftily dodge trash and the like all over the ground, left there by negligent persons. I also need to be wary and alert for parking meters, street signs, garbage cans, screaming blind children, rabid, playful animals and various flying objects whose only purpose in life is to interfere with my bike voyage.

As I ride I pass several people walking, some of them give a genial "hello" and I try to return the gesture with a gracious "nod" but am so frightened of running into things and people and falling and looking like a dope that I try not to take my eyes off the sidewalk.

Before I know it, I'm at the FastStop, not out of breath, legs not on fire. This store has a gas station with a car wash next door to it loaded with a multitude of SUVs, station wagons, sports cars, the works - apparently they have hours on Sunday - filled with passengers on vacation, heading someplace, or simply enjoying the summer and driving around aimlessly. The wintertime - which is, of course, my favorite time of year - keeps a lot of them indoors and cooped up. Hot weather and clear skies draws them out, like furrowed bears emerging from an unpleasant hibernation.

I park the bike on the side of the FastStop, instead of on the chewing gum and cigarette-ash stained bike rack because Seth's Cannondale - for some reason - does not have a chain on it anywhere (also, no helmet, which I believe is some sort of fineable offense). I decide not to take long inside for fear of it being stolen.

A lot of the FastStop's customers are buying iced drinks and large bags of tortilla chips and enamel-rotting candy and cartons of overpriced cigarettes while sorting though pockets filled with loose change and wrinkled bills. A few are taking a chance at the lottery, picking this number or that, or purchasing a rub-off that suggests you'll win "A $1000 a week for the rest of your life *" with that little " * " representing a colossal paragraph in miniscule print which contradicts the former statement.

I quickly grab today's newspaper near the front window by the magazines, some Advil (they've run out of Tylenol, how convenient) and an 8oz cup of regular coffee, two half-and-halfs, two sugars.

Outside I sit by the bike, leaning against the grubby, spray paint stained easternmost wall of the store, sipping the stale coffee (which mostly likely was made some six-odd hours ago), reading the Classifieds. I figure: either I read it here or on the balcony of my apartment with Capo-In-A-Box, and as long as I have the coffee (to combat, tooth and nail, an impending headache that feels like it's chugging along and will eventually hit full steam in an hour or two) and free time and clear skies gloating above me, I figure, 'why not?'

It turns out that there are a significant number of jobs listed today more than several days ago when my fingers last had the privilege of touching inky, rough newspaper print.

There are two that get special notice from me: one is for the head coordinator of St. Jermaine Church. The job position entails technical and organizational skills, such as bookkeeping, computer database entry, word processing, management of a small staff. It requires setting up and maintaining a robust church schedule, arranging funerals, weddings and the like (I have always equated the two). I can only hope the pay is good (hopefully in the ballpark of what I make now), and features full-benefits (health, life, dental after thirty days), but unfortunately it requires "weekend work," a severe liability considering weekend time is time for me. It has a number you can call, which I intend to do tomorrow.

The second ad that I pay special attention to is consistent with this 'ironic' leitmotif. Apparently, the local area school district is hiring, come September (only a month and change away) what they refer to in the ad as "Emergency Substitute Teaching Positions." It doesn't require any M.A.'s or Ph.D.'s or specialized B.A. in Elementary Education, just a plain old Bachelor's Degree. It involves teaching at all the public schools in this area (K-8) and also the local high schools (not exactly ideal) but pays over $100 a day after putting in a number of months. I'm presuming I'll start at around $70 a day, which is less than what I make now (by a good deal). I'm not sure how this would settle in with my parents, as Mom didn't sound too keen on my leaving for less money and both my acquaintances thought leaving an easy job is downright moronic. I figure: what's the harm in trying? I could always turn them down, if offered. Anyway, I will call them tomorrow.

Sweating from the 1-2 punch of hot coffee causing slight cramping in my stomach and the UV rays being absorbed by my epidermis I wrap up the paper and swallow two Advil, and get back on the bike to return home. When I get back I will clean up the bike to cover my tracks, and, while I'm at it, feed Capo.

8.

Preston is telling me this morning all about his trip to Atlantic City for the weekend to gamble - his wife, apparently, finds enjoyment in such things. He suggests I go once just to see the place and walk around the boardwalk and just jump into the ocean, but I tell him no, none of that's for me.

I ask him what his son Kyle thought of it.

"Oh, we didn't take him. He stayed at Anisa's mother's house. We didn't really think there'd be much to do for him there, you know, only a few rides and he doesn't like walking around. Doesn't like those shows or comedians, can't swim. And neither of us wanted to take him out of school. But we did get these messages on the hotel phone, three, I think ... no ... yeah, yeah, and they were all about how, now what did he do? He, oh, he was - I think he, she said he was playing with the stove."

"What?"

"It's not a gas stove, it's doesn't have those coils that heat up, it's like there are just flat discs that turn bright orange. And him and his younger brother were crawling around on top and, what, and I think one of them turned it on and, she wasn't sure how, but neither got burned or anything like that, thank God."

"Why was he crawling on the counter?"

"Yup. He does that a lot, though."

"Crawl on things?"

"Crawl on, you know, the floor, yeah."

"Why?"

He shrugs.

"Better you than I," I say.

"You need kids, though," he tells me, "you can't grow up without 'em. You don't realize you're aging until you see them aging. They're a reflection of you."

Before I walk to the elevator, I opt to head back and inform Preston of my new job prospects.

"Do you really want to work for a church?" he immediately asks.

"If the pay's okay and they want me."

"Do you know what they pay?"

"Neither says exactly."

"What kind of expenses you have?"

"Car, apartment, ummm, phone, that sort of thing."

"Go for it," is all he tells me, "as long as it pays enough."

I use the elevator and carefully make my way to my desk, not having to speak to anyone or explain my lateness, as the hallways are vacant and freshly vacuumed, with no small fragments such as hole punchings or staples or slivers of paper tainting the perfect pattern splayed out beneath me. When I do get to my desk/workspace and past the only person in the entire area with me, Brenda the Errand Girl (I don't know if that's her name or if that's what she does, but she appears to be in all places and all floors at all times, delivering this, organizing that, keeping irate parties content, transporting small machinery from one area to another). She looks up at me, and then down, back at a stack of what seems to be blank printer paper on top of a four-wheel cart she's pushing around.

On my desk, I find that those at Network Services are much more efficient that I originally presumed - my brand new computer is sitting on my desk, replacing the finger-grease and dust-ridden abacus that previously belonged there. There's a cream-colored monitor, a cream-colored tower, a cream-colored keyboard, a cream-colored mouse, a cream-colored mouse pad and - oddly enough - a small green plant resting next to my LCD clock, which reads 8:40 AM. I immediately inspect the odd little creature, which is tiny but very pretty. My Aunt Caroline (on my mother's side) had always been a plant person - she filled her cramped, two-room apartment with dozens and dozens of exotic plants, which she claimed helped her with her asthma problems, but I question the validity of such an assessment (it recalls Che Guevera's belief that smoking cigars helped with his chronic breathing difficulties). Safe to say she's dead (and has been for two years now), and so, of course, is he.

Inside the potting soil is a toothpick with a small piece of lined paper impaled on it - it reads, in pencil:

"A fern is a rhizome"

Was the plant simply placed here by mistake? There are no signatures or names on it, no eyewitnesses around to verify. I don't bother to ask around since there isn't anybody else to ask (if there were they would most likely be as dumfounded as I). I decide to simply enjoy the presence of this silent little wonder, and claim it for my own.

I don't bother turning on the sparkling new PC and opt to dive straight into phone calls - the numbers of the two jobs I circled in the paper.

I try the church number first. It rings four times before anyone picks up.

The voice coming from the other end of the line is raspy but feminine (more accurately, it sounds like a man imitating a woman's voice) and belongs to Sheila, the Church Receptionist. I tell her who I am, and what I want, and request information about the position.

"They didn't tell me much about it, so I really don't know," she informs me, obviously kept out of the loop (her phone number is the one listed in the paper).

"Well, can you tell me what the pay is like over the phone? Can you tell me what the hours would be?"

"You'd have to speak to Father Kusta about that - I really don't know."

"Is he there?" I ask.

"No, he's at the hospital."

"Can I leave a message for him?"

"You can, but he probably won't get back to you for quite some time, he has a very busy week planned. Did you send in a resume?"

"No."

"You have to do that first."

"Well I just wanted to know what the position is about before I send anything."

"After we receive it, we'll review it and then call you."

"Do you know when the interviews will be?"

"No, we'll call you," she repeats.

"That's all I need to know, fine, thanks, bye," I grumble, and hang up the phone.

I'm not pleased with the lack of information I'm supplied with but I will punch up a copy of the old resume nevertheless, and give it a shot. I could type up the resume now, but decide to wait to do it on the IBM typewriter I have back at the apartment.

The second phone call is to the School District Human Resources Department. The girl who answers mumbles her name and I have to think for a moment before starting in with the typical "Hello, I'm interested in...."

The woman on the other end seems to know more than the last lady, which is obviously a relief to me.

"For the Emergency Substitute Position you need to fill out the Application Forms from us and submit them by

August 21st." I figure, with the quickness of her answer that she's been asked this a lot today.

"What if they aren't in by then?" Just want to be safe.

"Well, it takes a while for it all to get processed and you want to start at the beginning of the school year, don't you?"

"Yes, ma'am," I reply.

"You also need to get a Criminal Check and a Child Abuse Check sent from the state capital, but everything you need to know is explained in the packet."

"When can I pick it up?"

"Whenever you'd like to, we're open until 4:30 PM today." She sneezes hard and says "excuse me."

"Allergies, right?"

"Hmm?"

"Seasonal allergies?"

"Cold."

"I see. I'll … can I stop by today?"

"That's fine. Do you know where we are?"

"Brownleaf Street, right?" I'm reading it right out of the ad.

"That's it. Just stop by Human Resources and ask the girl at the desk for the packet."

I thank her for her help and hang up.

Not entirely eager to settle down to work or typing out anything or doing much (or even turning on the new machine sitting in front of me) I take out the yellow notepad from my top-left desk drawer and spend a good deal of time doodling on it and trying to draw a semi-accurate picture of my new plant, but can't seem to get the proportions right and my representation either looks too fat or too tall, too slanted or too sloppy. My heart goes out to you, master painters.

Frustrated at my artistic ineptitude I put the pad away and set out to break in my virgin PC. With a push of the appropriate buttons, it springs to life, purring softly and delicately like a fine-tuned automobile. The keyboard isn't filthy and the mouse is smooth to slide around as it has a lint-and-germ-free pad beneath it. The screen is clearer and less abrasive on my eyes than its predecessor, which seemed streaked and smudgy from being sprayed with furniture polish despite warnings in the form of stickers placed on the machines by the company pleading for them not to touch. Ah, those Office Cleaners. Ignoring requests and instructions as always. I remember back when I was one and how I looked forward to it. I would make sure to not only *not* do what was requested, but to add a piece of antagonism into my sly/juvenile revenge/assault, by going through desk drawers and doing little things to bother people. On noted occasions I would go through their desk drawers for files and shred and toss them away in the dumpster out back before I'd get caught. I was also fond of deleting key files/directories off their personal computers, out-right formatting their hard drives and snapping apart 3 ½ inch diskettes with backup information on them. Once or twice, I can't quite remember, the individual had prescription pills in their desk drawer (I don't recall the name), and I flushed them and filled the translucent orange container with Tylenol from another desk. For most people - whether they wrote bad notes or not - I went through their personal belongings, just to read the notes their husbands/wives/offspring/co-workers wrote for them in birthday/holiday cards, fished through their computer files for questionable material. More often than not I found little of interest. But all that was youthful nonsense....

By 1 PM, I get ¾ of the work done, chugging away on claims stacked neatly in the wire bin on top of the desk, each ranging from deviated septum to rhinoplasty or breast reduction or gastric stapling and so on and so forth. One individual, and I can't figure out the details, sent a photo of his face, about half of which (I'm approximating) is covered by some gigantic, disfiguring mole that he wants removed (was he born with it? did it just *appear*?). Frankly, I can't say I blame him. While I think about this, I get to thinking about the role of the dermatologists, and how they are able to wake up every day (or oncologists, or proctologists, or general practitioners) and look at the most horrid of things, and still be able to go home and not be completely affected by any of it. Perhaps they are less sensitive to such flaws as someone like myself. I always figured it was merely desensitization, weaving its magical spell.

I decide to go to the break room and make myself a cup of Instant Coffee, in packet form, which I actually don't find even remotely palatable but it's the only kind of coffee in there - the giant Bunn machine was confiscated, reportedly by a different floor who had broken theirs somehow (I knew about this from a note left in the vacant spot - where the Bunn formerly sat - by some incredibly disgruntled caffeine addict, presumably male, reading: "WHOEVER TOOK IT, YOU HAD BETTER BRING IT BACK OR THERE WILL BE BLOODY FUCKING HELL TO PAY," unaware that this gesture is entirely in vain, as the thieves will most likely never return to the room or get caught). One day, I overheard a conversation between Brenda the Errand Girl and Mr. Thomas, and they were verbally drawing out all the possibilities - from Human Resources to Customer Service to the People On Floor Two to the Cleaning Crew - like an amateurish Holmes and Watson. Tsk, tsk, my ambitious sleuths - it appears as if Moriarty has had his/her way with you.

I find in one of the cupboards a brand new pack of Styrofoam cups, which I break open. There's already some "unused" cups face down, unwrapped, stacked on top of each other, but I figure if I can get a fresh one - why not? As I fill it up with hot water from the red faucet on the Cloister water cooler and pour the coffee packet in, Mr. Thomas walks in the room with another gentleman who is wearing a generic gray polo shirt and khaki Dockers - Mr. Thomas, a straw hat and sandals. This man is approximately the same height as Mr. Thomas and roughly the same age (early 30s) but sports rapidly thinning blonde hair. Mr. Thomas immediately breaks off whatever he was saying to the other man and turns to me.

"So what are you up to?" He opens up the refrigerator and takes out an apple that I could have sworn I saw last week.

"Just resting my eyes."

He makes a 'deflated' sound with his mouth. "Don't work so damn hard! Relax. Oh, here - this is Clive Metzger, he's new and working with me in Marketing. Clive - this is Devon, who works in-"

"I do everything here."

They both laugh. I follow along.

We shake hands. His sinewy claw completely envelops my frail mitt.

"Nice to meet you" we both say, simultaneously, trained from birth to do so, the social custom engrained in both of us.

Mr. Thomas throws away the half-eaten apple, making a bizarre facial grimace that tells me that yes, it was the apple I saw in there some time ago.

"Well." Mr. Thomas says, heading towards the door, "we're off. I'm giving him a small introductory tour, showing him all the
departments-"

"It'll take you all day," I interrupt.

"Yeah, gotta go," he says and they both take off, continuing their conversation.

Mr. Thomas is not my boss, but I consider him my superior even though I'm technically not in his department - he's the only one on the whole floor who says anything to me (he's pretty much the only one I ever consistently see, for that matter).

I've noticed people react positively to Mr. Thomas, and I guess it's because he's so extroverted and comfortable - if that is a suitable term - to be around. His radiating charm is astounding, even though he's important in this company's hierarchy. Yes, I have considered this to be a front, of sorts, and thought about how the act could be intentionally designed to mislead others in confiding in him, but I can't tell whether he's fake or genuine and don't like wasting any mental energy taking him apart.

I squander the next two hours of the day sipping the Instant Coffee, which goes from hot to lukewarm to cold to undrinkable in about an hour, and finish up some random paperwork. Since all of the assignments are completed, at 4 PM I duck out, and find my way to the car. If asked where I was, I'd simply say I skipped lunch.

I have never been very good with directions, and I make two wrong turns - one at Dunne, the other at Bradford - before I get my bearings and eventually find the School District's main headquarters on Brownleaf Street, which is an old-fashioned stone building two stories high with a colossal football field right in its backyard. I've lived in this town all my life - you'd think I could find my way around better. My lack of driving experience and indifference to street names renders me virtually useless when it comes to finding new locations and arriving on time, and it's a good thing I left work when I did.

There's a medium-sized parking lot across the street almost completely filled with compact cars of all styles and models - Hyundais and Geo Metros mixed with BMWs and Audis, all of them shimmering and clean, as if a car wash were nearby, or the School District paid someone to hose down the whole lot.

Noticing the "Entrance" sign, I make my way in easily, and straight through the dual doors that are propped half-open, presumably to let some air circulate through the building (it is a bright, warm day with no overcast). Once in, I see a "Human Resources" sign, with a confident brown arrow showing me the way. There are other signs scattered meticulously about the winding hallways, ensuring you don't get lost, several dozen feet away from each other. I pass down several halls and through several doors and past metal garbage cans and ferns that need to be watered and offices filled with folks on phones, using ballpoint pens or just plain chitchatting.

Before I know it, I arrive in front of the Human Resources door, with a chestnut wood sign fastened onto it, decorated with Gothic-style bright yellow/gold lettering:

Human Resources
Hours: M-F, 8:00 AM - 4:30 PM

I turn the brass knob and slowly creak the door open, as if I were trying to avoid a grand entrance. Standing about five feet away from the door is a middle-aged woman with a purple silk blouse and high-heels with a stack of multi-colored papers, her left side facing me.

She turns to look. "Yes?" she asks.

"I wanted to pick up a, I think it's a 'packet' for the Substitute Teaching Position in the paper. Someone on the phone told me to come here - I hope I'm not too late." I check my watch: 4:24.

"Oh no, we usually stay a little longer than 4:30. Wait, I'll get the materials for you."

She sets down the paperwork and walks off.

I notice, while standing close to the doorway to the department how tidy and organized everything appears to be. There doesn't seem to be any visible clutter, empty cardboard boxes, heaping piles of trash, useless and outdated computer technology, boxes of software in stacks, miscellaneous photocopies strewn about. I interpret this organized office as a sign of efficiency, but it could also be due to a stark-raving mad superintendent, juiced up on herbal supplements and hell-bent on order, it's tough to say.

The Receptionist/File Organizer arrives from another room with a manila folder just for me.

She opens it up to explain everything to me, which I only half-hear. "This is the background information. Your schooling history, awards and such go here. This-" she flips through, "-is your physical paper. And these-" flip again, "-are your Criminal and Child Abuse checks. You need to send them in, along with two $10 money orders to the state capital. It takes a while, but they should be back in two weeks. Also, this here asks you for an Essay. It should be a page long. And here-" more flipping, "-this is the application for your Emergency Teaching Certificate. It's another $15, sent to the state capital."

"For the essay, should I type it?"

"Hmm?" She looks up. She is standing entirely too close to me, but I force myself not to budge.

"The essay. Should it be typed?"

"If you want. But nothing else has to be."

"I see-" nodding, "When is all this due?"

"As soon as you can get it in."

"All right," I say, accompanied by more nodding. "Thanks for your time."

"You do know this lasts only a year, right?"

"Certainly, yes."

"I just wanted to make sure you knew."

I quickly dash out of the building, now going in the opposite direction from where the arrows are pointing, clearly avoiding their guidance, and thereby leaving the premises. Across the street I spot my black Honda and drive home, the application riding in the passenger seat, right next to me. The next step: start gathering information.

I mull it over as I eat Uncle Ben's Instant Rice slightly stained by Kikkoman Lite Soy Sauce and smothered with steamed broccoli and two sides: a baked potato, dry, and canned corn (with no salt added). I normally don't go vegetarian often, and didn't have anything substantial for lunch (only the bad coffee and a butterscotch hard candy I found in my desk drawer, left there eons ago). I figure: I can lie my ass off on the Essay, forge the physical, get the Criminal and Child Abuse checks cleared, and then send off for the certificate and be on my way.

But there is something in the packet the lady forgot to mention: a paper in here requesting three references be submitted in written form (they just can't be called, it stipulates). That's magnificent. Who am I supposed to put down? My parents are out - they don't accept family. Amy and Seth are out - they hardly say anything to me. Sterling and Davis? Maybe, but who can be the third? I contemplate just making them up - writing under three unique nom de plumes, each recommendation overflowing with convivial adulation - but decide to ask around before I do that.

While I'm corralling all this personal information, and thinking about possible courses of action, I realize I need to exhume all 15-20 odd pounds of the rotting IBM Correcting Selectric III I have in a box someplace and punch out a fresh resume (copied, years ago, in loving homage, to the resume Sterling made for himself - I borrowed the same format and structure and "Objectives" from him, only changing the personal details. He, naturally, let me copy freely, as he himself borrowed the format from someone else. I do need to update it slightly, as these last few years must be accounted for.

I find the archaic machine in my kitchen closet/pantry, in a cardboard box that formerly held Grade A Eggs. My old resume is in the filing cabinet, second drawer. As I review it, I wisely decide to wipe out some of the more ludicrous parts, which I can't believe I included. For the OfficeClean blurb in there, under "Job Duties" I wrote: "Cleaned up and managed work environment for slovenly workers." Why on Earth did I include that I worked there, anyway?

I heft the clunky typewriter onto the kitchen table, relocating the half-used Vanilla Cookie candle (the label on it says it can last up to 150 hours) to the kitchen counter, and sit down with a cup of hot green tea, the old resume and some blank paper and get ready to work.

The scent emanating from the innards of the light-brown typewriter is faint - almost scentless (there's a slight whiff of lubricant, that's all) - but it still works properly, with the keys and frame being minimally dusty. You'd think they'd stick after all these years of use and abuse at Mom's law office - she used it before the 286s (!) came out. Since then she'd pushed aside this old sage sitting beneath my fingertips in favor of its more sprightly offspring, which, for her benefit, had the ability to save documents, which, in turn, saved precious time (she'd kept the typewriter to do envelopes only for a while). Today she and her two Secretaries (or Paralegals, or Personal Assistants, whichever) are equipped with state-of-the-art computers and the latest in word processing software, and brought the unwanted, inconvenient, 20-some-year-old IBM typewriter home and tossed it in the cellar to forget about and clear away. Before I relocated here, I had salvaged the machine to type my Journal entries. It has stayed with me ever since, even though I do not use it for the reason I brought it over here (I am not only a shabby typist, but also a sloppy writer and constantly need to make corrections or alterations or scratch this out or move this paragraph, etc.).

The clicking goes on for a little while as I cautiously alter and edit my former resume, fixing errors, briefly describing my current work experience and basically lying my fool ass off. I figure I'm either too youthful or not experienced enough (or both) and it's a complete waste of time. I question my own reasoning as to why any of this matters.

The spacing appears to be off on the finished product, as the left margin is about 1" wide while the right is .5", and the typing paper must have been crooked because the text leans only *slightly* to the left, but I figure "No matter" and rummage through kitchen drawers for an envelope and a book of stamps, both of which I discover in the same exact place (right by the scissors, masking tape and hole puncher). I type the envelope - which is supposedly the professional way of sending these things out in the world (complete with an "ATTN: Father Kusta" in the lower left-hand corner) - fold the resume, seal it, stamp it and set it aside.

Oh, and I did forget to mention that on the resume I added that I worked as an Altar Boy for three years for the Church my parents belong to. It can't possibly hurt.

The Emergency Substitute Position is a much more daunting application/task, as there's infinitely more to send than just a crummy old resume. The more into the material I read, the more I find I need to provide. Apparently a transcript from my university is required for proof I went to school there (why don't they simply call the place themselves? Or do they want to huddle in a small circle and mull over why I received a "D" in Political Science, PS121, "The Writings and Views of James Madison?"). I make a note for myself to call the Registrar sometime tomorrow (during work) to take care of that tiny fragment.

It's paper completion time now, as I sift through the folder to find the simplest forms to fill out first with a black medium-size Bic pen which I gnawed - in particular the cap and the top of the shaft - to bits. The General Application and the Emergency Certificate Agreement are both simple, requiring only a few basic bits of info, asking whether or not I am a US Citizen, ever convicted of a crime other than minor traffic violations, had licenses revoked in the past and things of that nature. Then there's the Standard Application, slightly different, which asks for the general stuff (name, SS#, areas of certification and the like) as well as personal references, work experience, and whether I've been convicted of a crime or not. On one of the pages there's the (aforementioned) Essay that I need to jot down. It asks that it be written as briefly as possible. It gives you a choice - you can pick to write about one of the following:

1. What are the most important aspects to classroom instruction?
2. How can new forms of technology be successfully integrated into the classroom?
3. Explain personal beliefs regarding student discipline.
4. Give your views on an ideal classroom.

Right. Number 3 is what can best be described as a trap, as the individual who chooses that one had better be extremely careful in his/her phrasing; any slight ambiguity in the essay and he/she will be most likely questioned on it. I, for one, will avoid that one.

I decide to save the essay until last, as it will take some time to compile and I want to finish the rest of this mess before 9:30 PM (in an hour or so) so I can continue leafing through my tattered paperback, *The Penguin Dictionary of Quotations,* and pick out my favorite dead authors, shower and sit outside until about 1 AM or so, and savor the reduced temperatures and welcome breeze.

The "Personal Health Record," or physical paper, looks like a challenge, indeed, as it's filled with ambiguous medical phrasing that I can't make out and that the medical journals stacked neatly on my one bookshelf can't tell me how to forge them (if I were on the Internet I'm sure I could find something on there to tell me - or, at least, that's what *Time* suggests). I decide to wing it, and do the old "Doctor's Print" technique of scribbling letters that look more like Sanskrit than anything remotely English. The "markings" are a lot of waves and dashes and smudge marks, and my "4's" look like "q's" and my "8's" like "B's" and the "1's" are all "l's" (frankly, the whole thing is a clownish caricature). I make sure to scribble in all the blanks for the tuberculosis test and immunization record, putting checks and slashes where I can't think of anything else. I make up dates for the shots - 12/20, 11/21, 5/7, 3/30 - and put large slashes through all the "Normal" boxes (versus "Abnormal") and more large slashes through all the "No's" for whether or not I have cardiac problems, diabetes, skin disorders and top off this sketchy smorgasbord with a big loopy signature, which is simply an "M" and a "B" with squiggly lines trailing from the ends and when asked to print the name I put down "Dr. Mark Bagovich" and some random address in Delaware (2344 E. 11th Street) which I doubt exists. If asked why he isn't located there, I'll simply tell them he moved to Seattle to start a new practice or maybe over to England to pick fruit. And if they want it done over, I'll do the same thing again, only next time with blue ink.

And in case you're wondering, the real life Mark Bagovich, last I heard some four years ago, was somewhere in the Middle East flinging SmartBombs at anything that moves.

While they look mean and deathly serious, the Criminal Record Check and Child Abuse History Clearance are a snap to fill out - more addresses, more dates of birth, more social security numbers. The papers say the state should return them in roughly four to five weeks, though I am skeptical and figure it will most likely take longer.

And that's the end of *those* papers. I've saved the best for last. The Essay:

I've decided to eliminate two of the topics right off the bat for logical reasons (2 & 3), I am completely speechless when it comes to 4 (ideal classroom? Are they asking if I'd like a sauna and Jacuzzi and bed in there? Are they asking about what type of children I'd like to have in there, as if children could somehow be radically different than the way they've always been?), so am stuck with the first one. It's the most open-ended of all of them, and the easiest one to get out quickly (I was going to go the Joycean route of relying on my stream of consciousness but the 'stream' in me is but a mere rivulet and, more important, I am not, nor can ever be, Mr. Joyce).

I figured I could take this piece of personal opinion and literary bombast and go one of the following ways: (a.) being either deeply sarcastic or (b.) painfully honest. Pulling out my own shiny bullshit-o-meter, this is what I come up with, after writing a rough draft on scrap paper first and making corrections:

Learning & You: It's *Not* To Be Reckoned With

I believe I am uniquely qualified to teach in your school district because, above all, I see youth as preeminent examples of what Locke referred to as 'tabula rasa' - blank slates - waiting to be 'written over' with material of all sorts, enhancing their brains and minds with English skills, mathematical aptitude, scientific formulas and truth - as well as other aspects of life worth covering such as social fortitude and career-related verisimilitude.

If the educator (or parent) fails him or her (meaning, the child) in providing intellectual stimulation - from a young age - the child never acquires the thirst - the rapt enthusiasm - for knowledge. They grow up and evolve rejecting school because the information being taught isn't sinking in; they become bitter, hostile, get poor grades and can develop low self-esteem and low self-worth. This downward spiral is to be avoided at all costs, and it starts when they are young.

Teachers need to be kind, caring, sympathetic to the child(ren)'s needs. They need the gift of patience - which I possess - as well as the ability to make things compelling and interesting. No child wants a dull instructor speaking in monotone, behaving in an aloof manner, indifferent to their needs and wants. Education does not have to be "dull" or "boring." It is the job of the educator to act interested, and subsequently keep the children interested.

As a potential educator, I feel I need to encourage focus, guidance and participation. Interaction with peers in a monitored way promotes group skills and social acceptance. The children should be able to look to each other to lend them a much-needed hand when confusion or trouble arises. Teamwork, and positive teacher-student interaction are healthy ways for both parties - student and instructor - to grow.

And grow we must.

After rereading this for thrills I throw it away and write something less mock-glorified and idiotic. I debated with myself in myself as to whether or not underlining the last line was excessive. But they'll take it at face value, because they understand nothing of sarcasm and don't realize that their *product* - children - will either grow up to be geniuses or failures. It's all in the cards, my acquaintances.

9.

I slept last night under a precipitation-less blanket of black on my balcony, right next to Capo who tussled around a bit when I accidentally kicked the box but was, for the most part, calm. Inside it was entirely too stuffy and I was comfortable, in my blue bathrobe, on the green and white striped lawn chair, feet propped up, head askew, outside. Amazingly enough, it was a relaxing spell, until 5 AM when Amy, leaving for work, startled me (I didn't realize grocery store shifts started so early - perhaps the cereal aisle needed to be rearranged in alphabetical order or the produce squeezed). The noise she produces is enough to wake up everyone within a square mile, with the apartment door slamming, car door slamming and loud rock music playing from inside the automobile, combined with the fact that she lets her car - an '89 Ford *something* - idle for so very, very long. You'd never think such a little woman could be so damned disruptive (when I'm inside I've actually gotten used to it and been able to sleep through it). Today, to make sure I was up for reveille, she knocked over a garbage can directly below where I was resting, peacefully. Disturbed and irritated I then proceeded to stumble my way back inside (so dazed I neglected to close the balcony door) and collapsed, eyes completely shut, on my mattress, without rearranging pillows or mustering the strength to cover myself with a blanket. The real alarm went off at 7:55 - just in time for me to take another shower, shave (once, twice, three times against the grain, nicking my skin twice and becoming enraged at the blood slowly coming out, but growing calmer after I applied the styptic pencil, causing the wound to coagulate) and eat.

I had spent a good deal of time last night listening to a baseball game on the radio (the Red Sox were playing Baltimore) and drawing up a mental list of potential references. Essentially, I had narrowed it down to three people who may not know me well, and may be willing to write small, brief, "Yeah, he's pretty decent" or "I trust him with my heart and soul" or "He's a loyal fellow!" Nothing elaborate - I'm not asking for Proust, here - but something tactful and concise that they'll accept and think highly upon. I don't know anyone that could provide me with a detailed pat-on-the-proverbial-back from college or high school, so I'm a little stuck there. As always, though, I can open up Plan B and write them *for* them.

The three are: Preston, Mr. Thomas and Marie, Davis' girlfriend (and a certified R.N. to boot!). I haven't spoke to any of them for long periods of time or engaged in deep, probing, personal discussions, and only ate lunch with Marie twice (never with Preston or Mr. Thomas), but figure they can scrape something together.

I'll need to call Marie sometime later - from my apartment, regretfully, as she's most likely at work today (nurses have incredibly odd hours, from what I am told). I don't know why I decided on her - perhaps it's because I know of no other females, and she's the only one that tries hard to listen to me. Last we spoke was during Davis' birthday party - in March, I believe - held at her home in wealthy suburbia. While there were plenty of people there - people from the engineering company Davis works for, other people he met at Villanova, family, gypsies, vagabonds and other characters I didn't know, a great number of Marie's friends and co-workers, Sterling's friends, Eric, and people we went to high school with and I had to prepare a brand new, shiny personal narrative to keep them "abreast" on what I am doing with my life and where I've been for all these years. I only went to that "gathering" because Marie called and pleaded for me to go - or, not pleaded, but *asked ... kindly* - and submitted to my own fellow-feeling and gave in, rationalizing that I should, out of formality and custom. Marie's charm and motherly "I know how it is" demeanor works wonders on me, and for some reason she enchants me and I find myself swept away by her sheer honesty. She was telling me about ghastly burn victims and gunshot wounds and I kept pumping her for juicy bits of icky *insider* information on what this procedure is like that I read about in this journal or that book and I never sensed that she was put off by my prodding and seemed to find some joy in conveying knowledge to me.

I got to work extremely late due to a combination of heavy traffic - there was a funeral procession tying up the works with enough cars to fill all the lots in Disney World - and personal matters (I had to get the three money orders for the Criminal Check and Child Abuse Check and Certificate Fees). For some reason, Preston wasn't at his front desk - I fear he may have the day off, or potentially the week off - and intend to check back later.

At around 10-ish I phoned the registrar at my old school (thank goodness I kept the School Phone Directory from my Senior Year in the filing cabinet back at the apartment). I basically got a lot of "yesses" and "okays!" from the woman on the other end of the connection, who asked for my Social Security number and current address and said they'd send it as soon as humanly possible, and I asked if they could get it out by tomorrow and she was like "yeah right okay" and I said "fine" and "goodbye" and "thanks" - but not in that order - and hung up. Then, minutes later, I got worried that they were paying me lip-service and got to thinking that they don't send things to anyone unless that someone sends them a form or proof of who he/she is so then I call back and then they're telling me everything's perfectly fine and I shouldn't worry and that all they needed was my Social Security number.

———

Letter #1

The work in the wire rim basket is high, but I don't touch any of it - I decide to find Mr. Thomas for fear he may wander out of the office, building or the like and go work out or jog on this fine, warm day with sweat and sunshine intermingling everywhere outside, forming a formidable brew. I spend some time wandering around my floor, but get lost in a sea of carpet and cream-colored walls and hazel doors and few - if any - signs. I eventually make contact with Brenda the Errand Girl, looking poised and confident in a jet-black blouse and matching knee-length dress, lips completely coated with a dark purple/violet lipstick, hair pulled all the way back into a little knot fastened right over the occipital lobe on the back of her head. She's carrying an adding machine in both her arms - its cord completely blends in with her mute attire. I stop her dead in her tracks.

"I'm sorry-" (I always start apologetically for everything, but to me it's a sign of humility and earnestness), "-but do you have any idea where a Mr. Thomas has his office? I think he works in Marketing."

She squints to look at me. "Who?" she asks.

"Thomas," I reply.

"I'm not sure who you're talking about, but Marketing is down *that* hall," she points, "to the right, down the second corridor on your left, then the first door on your right. The Receptionist will know who you're looking for." She then starts to march off, possibly irritated, her forward progress has been halted and time wasted.

"W-w-wait. First door on right, right?" (I told you I'm bad with directions.)

She stops. Pauses. Turns. "Don't you work on this floor?"

I look at her for a long time, squint back at her and then turn to go in the direction she pointed at without saying a word. I could have said something, but I would have only been wasting by breath - hostile words don't change anybody.

Like a nomad I wander and wander, without anyone else to ask, down vacant corridor after vacant corridor, aimless. Miraculously I do find my way to the door I think I want. On the front door there's a white piece of paper with the following printed in orange marker:

~~Sales (Section C)~~
Marketing (Section A)

... and I open the door and step in. The Receptionist, with hair like a poofy, blonde wig (perhaps it is a wig!) who is - appropriately - on the telephone, sees me enter but doesn't bother saying anything or giving me pseudo-ESL with her hands to tell me to "wait" or "hold on" or anything to that extent. She lets me stand there until she gets off the phone, writes something vital on a "While You Were Out" pad and then looks up at me.

"Yes?"

"I'm here to speak to this Mr. Thomas. I think he works on this floor, but I noticed on the door that this is sec-"

She interrupts. "Are you a client?"

"No. I work here too. In Claims. I just saw him not too long ago walking around this new hire."

"There is no person working in this department with a last name of Thomas," she informs me.

"There isn't?"

"No."

"Well...."

"What does he look like?" she asks, not amused, possibly thinking I'm playing games with her, which she is not in the need for.

"Always wears casual stuff, uh, straw hats, Bermudas. Wavy dark brown hair. Slight stubble. About, oh, 6, he's about 6 foot 2, 3. Nice guy."

"Does he have glasses?"

"No."

"Did you say goatee?"

"No, just, it's darker in that area." I run my right hand around my jaw.

She picks up the phone. "The person I think you're looking for is Mr. Daubens."

"Oh," I say, startled, "I must have misheard his name when I guess he or someone else mentioned it."

She talks into the phone, "Craig? There's a young, hold on, what's your name?"

"Devon."

"First or last?"

"First."

"There's a man here from claims named Devon here to talk to you." Pause. "Should I say you're busy?"

I interrupt, "Tell him it will take only five minutes."

She relays the information. "Right." Pause. "Now? Okay." She hangs up. "He can see you briefly right now. He has a team conference on floor two in a couple of minutes, so he can't talk forever."

"Thanks."

"Just sit down and he'll be right out."

There's only one available chair in the entire room, and it's right in front of her, so I don't have much of a choice as to where to park myself.

It isn't but two or three minutes that elapse until one of the doors behind the receptionist pops open and Mr. Thomas appears - as Mr. Daubens. This disappoints me on a personal level because I have always been exceptionally good at remembering people's names if nothing else (I am pitiful at recalling and having to describe faces).

He smiles, extends a hand, which I shake, reluctantly, and he invites me inside his cozy, ultra-comfortable office, which he refers to as his "den."

Inside there are dozens of black and white photos of ducks, bears, rivers and mountain ranges, all in fancy double-matted cherry wood frames. There's a gigantic fully painted and stained mallard in the left hand corner of the room that is tall (about two-and-a-half feet high) and must weigh a ton - it's easily larger than a Saint Bernard. When I ask him about it, he tells me his father made it: "He was an accountant, but his hobby was wood carving - this was his prized creation." His desk is glimmering and immaculate with only a small laptop and one single sheet of plain white paper on top. The lighting is dim and moody, and the distinct smell of jasmine incense burning (on a table to my direct right) puts you in a holistic mood.

Strangely though, there are no plants anywhere in his office - I concede that their presence might add to the "frontier-sy" mystique.

He inches towards the back of his desk, places both hands on top of his plush desk chair.

"How can I help you?"

"Well-" I hesitate, "- look, if you have to go I can always...."

"No," he interrupts. "Go on. Let them wait down there." He smiles.

I fidget slightly. "Well, I'm applying for this other job at...."

"Other job?" he interrupts (again).

"Yes, another job. There's an opening at the school district for a Substitute Teacher that I wanted. I mean, it's fine working here and all, but, I'm itching to move on."

"Right." He hunches over, takes his hands off the chair.

"And I wanted you to - I needed three letters of recommendation and wanted one from here. I has hoping you could write one for me."

He looks up. "But you don't work for me."

"I know, but, you know. I don't know who my boss is."

He laughs again, thinking I'm pulling his leg. "All right, but what do you need me to say?"

"Adjectives. You know. You're in Marketing. Sell me."

"Sell you?"

"Sell *me*."

He scratches the back of his neck. "I could, I can't do it now. I'll - I'll come up with something for you. Are you unhappy here?"

"No, it's I just want to, you know, try other things."

More thinking, on his part. He goes through his upper right-hand desk drawer for some mysterious object, shuffles things, closes it. "Do you want to work in this department? Here? I could make you a ... a ...."

"It's not that. Thank you but no."

He nods. "Well, all right. Give me some time and I'll come up with something and I'll mail it to you. How soon do you need it?"

"Whenever you get a chance, no rush."

"Okay."

He extends his hand again and comes closer to me from behind his desk. "Well, I'm not sure what else to say. You're a good guy, best of luck. Hopefully you'll be able to do something in the future that suits you better."

———

Letter #2

After he leaves the room and I leave my name and home address with his Receptionist I head down to the Atrium to see Preston. This time of day he is down there, reading the "Life" section of the USA Today. I tell him I need a huge favor.

"Are you in trouble?"

"Nothing like that. I need a letter of recommendation. I'm sending out resumes and applications and need references in case they ask."

"Why me?"

"Who else here am I going to ask? Just 10 minutes ago I asked another guy whom I would *just see sporadically* and had, 11 minutes ago, not even know the name of. All I need you to say is that I'm, I don't know. I'm 'honest.'"

"I don't have a computer here, I can't type."

"Do you have one at home?"

"Yeah, but only Kyle knows how to use it."

"Well, how about, how about I type up your recommendation now, upstairs, print it out, bring it down, and you approve it."

"You can't...."

"Come on! That's a good idea."

"And you'll bring it down."

"Yes."

"How soon?"

"Immediately."

"What are the people reading it going to make of 'Security Guard'?"

"I'll take care of that. Anyway, it shows I have range - from Executives to Nurses to Security Guards."

"H-hey. That doesn't make me sound too good, you know."

"And I scrubbed bathrooms for years."

He sighs. "Don't make it too long, though."

I assured him I wouldn't, and head up the elevator to type it on my PC. I construct the following, continuing the string of ridiculous bullshit that I've been producing of late:

To Whom It May Concern:

I have had the distinct and honorable pleasure of knowing this young man for an extended period of time - roughly two years - and worked with him on a regular basis. He has proven himself to be kind, thoughtful, creative and responsible. His determination would be an asset to your organization.

Signed,
Preston Szasz
Chairman of Security Services
... etc ...

"Well..." he says after reading it through. "Two years? Has it been two years?"

"Who keeps track? And what do you think of 'Chairman'?"

He smiles. "Whoever heard of that?"

"We just invented it."

———

Letter #3

Later, around 6:30, after I've eaten my Pizza-For-One and drank five cups if ice water (it promotes kidney health and presumably cleanses the skin), I call up Marie, and get her beeper. I hang up and sit by the phone, waiting patiently for her return call. I turn on WODE and listen to everything from Diana Ross to Bobby Vinton. I'm laying on the floor with a plush green pillow on my face and bags of ice on top of my feet. About an hour ago I fed Capo and changed his box, which was an oven inside.

It isn't until 7:14 that she rings back.

"I haven't seen you in a while," she tells me, "how are things?"

"Didn't Davis saying anything?"

"Does he ever?"

"How was Texas?"

"I'm guessing he didn't tell you that I got burned. Bad. I have fair skin and was too lazy to put on sunscreen and, you ever have it happen to you? The chills and all?"

"Nope. Say," disposing of small talk, "are you doing anything important?" I hear gurgling noises in the background and ask if she's using Scope.

"Ha ha ha! No! I'm boiling water. Gargling mouthwash, that's funny."

"I feel like I've been doing this all day. And I hate asking for favors."

"What?"

"I need a letter of recommendation from you, I'm going for this new job - hell, new jobs, if none of them pan out - and, you know how they ask for references?"

"Yeah?" The gurgling has stopped - now all I hear is an incessant *hummmmm* which makes it even harder to understand her, which in turn forces both of us to raise our respective decibel levels way up to avoid wasting precious phone time and potential misunderstandings (and a lot of "what?"'s)

"And I don't know many women, and I think it's neat that you're a nurse." I hope this doesn't get interpreted in any strange, derogatory way.

There's a pause, the humming is now accompanied by the sound of a faucet running and a "chopping" noise like horses trotting which could - perhaps - be some sort of food processor or mixer or Cuisinart or newfangled contraption. Marie has always seemed to be into the latest in kitchen technology (last Christmas I bought and mailed to her a knife collection from Farberware) and delves a good portion of her "free money" (money not spent on necessities) on home supplies (Davis was the one who tipped me off on this). "But Devon," she says, "I'm not sure I really know you enough to do that."

Ah-ha! The nefarious feminine lie. I've overheard this countless times in females dealing with males out there in the social jungle. Here's my juvenile breakdown: A certain male (let's call him 'XY'), is talking with a certain female (she'll be 'XX'). He doesn't pick up on signals well at all (or misinterprets them) and isn't aware that she is genuinely interested in another guy who's stronger, more fun, more intelligent (he will be 'XY/2') - who is basically into himself - and 'XX' is leaving herself open for 'XY/2's advance. So when 'XY' asks 'XX' for the possibility of a future 69, and is under the impression she is available when she really isn't she's waiting for this next big thing to happen, he gets 86'ed with "But I don't know you" (heavy linguistic emphasis on *know* - apparently 'XX' has no idea that in other cultures arranged marriages are *not* contingent on *knowing*, one learns that as one goes along) as an easier let down than (a.) Go away (b.) Are you coming on to me? (c.) I don't like you or (d.) Hey! You're not the next best thing!, after all of which 'XY' seriously needs a hug because his little morsel of hope and glimmering happiness has been whisked away by the wind.

However, my approach is *hardly* sexual and I refuse to back down. "Be creative," I say. "Stephen Crane never fought in that particular battle he wrote about in *The Red Badge of Courage*. Make something up. Be kind."

"Stephen Crane?" she asks. Now, along with the faucet and blender/mixer, there's also the sound of the microwave beeping and her breathing loudly into the cordless phone she must be walking around with. Combined, they form some sort-of avant-garde symphony that might impress Stockhausen.

"Listen," I raise my voice even higher, "Please. Do this. I'm serious. I'll owe you one."

"Owe me one?" There's a pause. "Fine, I'll come up with something. But, when, umm, do you need it?"

"The sooner the better."

She exhales hard. The microwave has stopped, as has the faucet. "But if they call, what should I say?"

"Just ask Davis."

"Why didn't you just ask him to do it in the first place?"

"You two should collaborate."

"All right. Look-" now, everything is silent, except for her breathing, "-we might be having a clam bake in sometime ... lessee..." rustling on her end, "in a few weeks. It's tentative - we might go to San Diego. But if we do have it, you have to come and you have to bring something."

"What kind of thing should I bring?"

"Food."

"Like a cake?"

"Well...."

"Because I can't cook."

"Try."

"I don't know...."

"Hey, I'm doing you a favor, here."

"Will you mail me the letter or not?"

She doesn't say anything and I hear silverware clatter.

"What's for dinner over there?"

"It's called, well, it's 'Dawn's Recipe.' It's a casserole that's made of fried onion rings and cheddar cheese and ground beef."

"Did Dawn give it to you?"

"Obviously."

Distracted and slightly bored I end the conversation.

"Do you want to come over to eat?" she offers.

"Thanks but no," I say and the conversation ends.

After I get off the phone I feed Capo and wash him off a bit in the shower, put him back in his box (he only tries to claw at me once), then engage in an exaggeratingly long shower myself, during which I take, once again, a precise and urgent mental note to never put myself in a situation where I have to ask others for anything. It's really too much for me, and them. Burdening others puts stress on my heart, my head - it's no good for me.

10.

As with all things, there is good and there is bad. August is a month that appears to contain both, and then some:

Positive.

Some diligent upstarts someplace, somewhere must be 'on-the-ball' (or whatever that blasted cliché is) as the Criminal and Child Abuse checks have shown up, in my tin mailbox (which is marked '3' to designate, yes, my floor number), both on exactly the same day (freakish, if I may say so), verified, stamped and processed. They said it would take 2-3 weeks, I was afraid longer (or not at all, considering, you know, *red tape*). So I am pleased to admit I am neither a Felon nor a Pedophile. Where's the confetti?

Not only that, but a little earlier on, Mr. Daubens and Marie's recommendations found their way into my hands, complete and quasi-professional (Marie's envelope has little balloon stickers and wide-eyed puppy dogs covering the back side, the letter gratefully does not). Daubens' mentioned how I would "laboriously toil" on "challenging tasks" and showed "dogged determination" in all I graced. He did mention how I was not employed by his department (the " * " in this case) but said if he had room he wouldn't have had to write the letter. The whole recommendation spans two stapled, double-spaced pages, on thick gray paper with the insurance company letterhead emblazoned, in full color, on the front page, covering ¼ of the space available. Impressive, I suppose.

Marie's is closer to reality, and made mention of how "quiet" and "private" and "reserved," but also how "smart" and "insightful" I can be. I can't tell if Davis had any say in it - there is a line about "willingness to explore new territory" which I find remarkably tongue-in-cheek - but appreciate the effort. At the bottom, her name and job title. At the top, the hospital logo.

Even stranger (yes, a lot of this *seems* detached, in a way) is how my alma mater, specifically, the registrar's office, managed to get, into my hands, my official transcript with no fees, no phone calls, problems or hassles just eight days after I phoned them! I recall years ago when I was enrolled there and had to argue with them virtually every damn semester because they were being stubborn, and didn't want to alter my schedule and shift around the aching, inconvenient Friday recitations to Thursday (I tried to avoid taking classes on Fridays so I could spend them in the basement of the campus library devouring several salami sandwiches and half-heartedly deciphering Bataille - or somebody like Bataille - in relative peace). They would always say, "But you don't *need* this moved" or "This requires the *professor's approval*" (which is illogical since the professor rarely - if ever - taught the recitations).

Either way, all the good fortune irks me because soon thereafter comes....

Negative.

I tried calling the Church I sent the resume to. Nothing.

I sent another resume to the Church. Nothing.

I called the chapel to get some information about the position. The response, from some teenage girl presumably getting minimum wage and saving up for that darling little pony she saw in the field: "Uhhh ... I don't know." (The word *know* is really dragged out here with a long "o" sound).

And, just as I feared, the clambake is on, and I've gotten several calls from both Marie and Davis reminding me to come (why, once again, I have no idea, but I interpret it as a sign of masochism on their part). I consistently ask as who exactly is going to be there and what is going to happen but neither commits to answering me and neither gives me a straight answer about anything. All they reiterate is the 'food' part, which yes, I do remember. And Davis mentions they bought a new TV set that I simply *have* to see.

I was going to try my hand at making the White Wine Gazpacho in the women's magazine that I saved in the top drawer of my filing cabinet, but examined the contents and figured that it's entirely too complicated to spend my time on (it isn't FORTRAN and could probably be figured out and made properly, but I am not gifted in the culinary arts and shan't try). Plus, I doubt whether anyone will want to have cold tomato soup in August, and I would be disappointed if no one ate it.

(Or, I could go the devious route and put strychnine or some other wonderful chemical in and pray they all eat it. I could simply leave it there and watch and laugh at every spoonful inhaled. But ah! I should not jest.)

I therefore, after some thinking, decide to go to the local grocery store and buy six or seven quarts of the turkey chili they make on the premises (or at least I am misled to thinking that) and dump them all into a large Tupperware container and bring that with me. It's tangy and spicy, but it is a hot dish and wonder whether or not it's appropriate. At least I don't have to make anything and be criticized.

The "Invitation" I received strongly suggested I arrive at 1 PM, so I strongly reply non-verbally by arriving two-and-a-half hours later, much to the chagrin of Marie, who makes mention of my tardiness the moment she opens the forest green door of her fully-landscaped, freshly mowed (each blade of grass trimmed to exactly the same height, no blade askew, as if the lawn got a buzz cut from the barber) and perfectly edged. It's on Vide Street, in a neighborhood predominantly occupied by (according to Davis, not I): Restaurateurs, Accountants, budding Entrepreneurs, Neurosurgeons and Jacuzzi-owning, basketball playing Public Defenders who are so out of shape and horribly uncoordinated that an unknowing onlooker might mistake them for tryouts for the Special Olympics. I've never seen them. Whenever I've been there - and this includes today - no other house in eye-or-ear shot is stirring.

Today, she is wearing a violet one-piece swimsuit covered by a large, loose-fitting white T-shirt, which hangs off her left shoulder. She is a tad displeased.

"Late?" I say, quasi-jokingly, "I got lost on my way over here."

"Riiight."

"Thank you for the nice letter." I get a dirty look complete with crinkled mouth and squinting eyes, hands on hips.

"What did you bring?" she asks.

"It's turkey chili. I made it yesterday." I hand her the Tupperware container, already pre-stained a light orange (as opposed to its proper color: clear) due to repeated use and purity-tarnishing tomato sauce.

She examines it from the side without struggling to pry off the blue lid. "Made it? It looks great. I'll put it out back."

"Should I?" I motion in-doors.

"You could have gone around back *that* way," she points to the side.

"But I want to see the new TV set that Davis mentioned on the phone." I lie, again.

"Oh, all right. Come on." She walks me inside.

Marie's house is clean and fragrant - it has a rose petal and talcum powder scent to it - and the walls are loaded with fake flowers and wooden baskets with ceramic trinkets inside and, my favorite, a huge, slightly pixilated framed photo of her with Davis taken in Niagara Falls, on the "Maid of the Mist." Davis is pretending to squeeze her to death while she has her head tilted back and mouth open, laughing. I never asked her about it.

We walk into a small, cramped room that should be spacious but is cluttered with a couch and bookshelves and the new TV, which she just turns on.

The set is massive - like a monolith - the image blinding, with it sitting a little too close to the couch in front of it to make it bearable (give it two more feet and it would be fine). The bookshelves are crammed with books and videocassettes and compact discs and records and a smorgasbord of every other imaginable trinket you can buy. I quickly scan her book collection and video collection but I have neither read nor seen any of them.

On the TV set is some man talking in front of a map of the United States and there are all these floating cartoon clouds and wicked lightning bolts sliding from state to state in a matter of seconds.

She says something but I don't hear it - I'm too focused on a stuffed animal that is face down on the one shelf. I lift it upright to get a good look - it's a cute monkey/orangutan with a mouth made out of string and long fuzzy arms and a thin tail - but when I let it go it falls back on its face.

"Oh!" she says, and takes the monkey/ape thing away.

"What is that?" I ask.

"I collect stuffed animals. Davis hides them on me."

"I see."

"Why don't you head outside? You can eat shellfish, right?"

"Sure."

"And there are baked potatoes and corn and other things. Go on and say hello to everyone."

"I will." Before walking out: "Nice TV."

"It better be."

As I venture out back and slide open the screen door I am presented with a spacious view of her entire back yard, which is wide and expansive.

For all the goodness that has been placed in my lap as of late, I suppose some badness tags along for the ride, as my request for cumulonimbus and thunderclouds and gray overcast and a cold front has gone unanswered. In cheerful irony, it's easily 100 - 102° outside, complete with a shiny and untainted sky. On the ground, in the enormous backyard, people are roaming everywhere - I'd estimate 60, maybe 70 (though, as usual, this may be off) - jumping in the giant peanut-shaped in-ground swimming pool that lies in the dead center of the whole yard (filled with splishy-splashy men and women and surrounded by sunbathers), laughing heartily, pacing around carrying clear plastic cups filled with Foster's or Miller Genuine Draft or Corona (all picked out by Sterling, I imagine, since those three are his personal 'Holy Trinity') and all-in-all enjoying the day. I, strangely, end up staring in blank oblivion at an inflated green sea horse in the in-ground pool that bobbles to-and-fro due to kicking and splashing and ripples (the pool is completely free of leaves, bugs and other debris and reminds me, a little, of the pictures of the waters in the Bahamas found in various vacation pamphlets and travelogues).

There are seven picnic-type tables set up to sit and eat at, and there are four other tables besides them parallel to the back of the house with random edible items: giant bowls of potato salad, crock pots filled with baked beans, baked ziti, meatballs, plates of corn, a gigantic bowl of Caesar salad, several kegs of beer, several coolers with cans of Coke, Sprite, Dr. Pepper and Pepsi inside. Behind the second of the many food-court-type tables is a tall cylindrical steamer being helmed by none other than Davis, sweaty-as-hell, in a white and blue checkered cooking apron and brand new Milwaukee Brewers hat. Sterling is sitting, sans shirt, at one of the picnic tables to my far-right, along with a girl I think we went to high school with but looks far more than and more muscular than I last recall (my mind/eyes could be playing tricks on me). Marie, meanwhile, shuffles over to Davis, hands him the Tupperware bowl of chili, says something, he laughs, sets it down and then she waves me over. I comply, because I'm not in the mood to stand in one spot for too long.

"Hey," he says, "don't you look at me like that. Bringing you here was her idea. I know you hate this."

I give a half-smile, "Well, it's free food. And, you know, a promise is a promise."

"You know we didn't think you were going to show," Marie says. This is (I think) the second time she's said something to this effect.

"Frankly, I didn't either."

"Well, you're just being the trooper then," she laughs.

Davis changes the subject. "You know you forgot your bumper sticker in the car the last time? I'll get it for you before you leave."

"Oh, I was tired and didn't remember where I left it."

Marie says she has to attend to something and walks away.

"You know," he tells me, as soon as Marie is out of ear-shot, "we were going to have a fucking tent set up, but Ms. Lazy over there didn't want to take the time to set it up and get it and, look - how many of her friends are here?"

I turn around, crinkle my neck, do a quick head count. "A lot?"

"How many, of all these people, do you think I know?" he asks.

"Half?"

"Less."

"A quarter?"

"About ten."

"Isn't that about a quarter?"

"Something like that. At least at my birthday there were more of my friends there," he says.

"Didn't she let you invite them this time?"

He doesn't answer.

"Can I get some of those clams?" I ask. He nods and prepares me a Styrofoam dish (decorated with colorful flowers) with a bag of clams (in their own moist net) on it, their mouths gaping open and facing the sky. Beside them he puts a Dixie cup of melted butter and some crackers.

"But did you see who's sitting there next to Sterling?" He hands me the dish, which I take with both hands.

"Isn't she-?"

"Yup. It's Annie Chapman. I think she's been on a workout regimen because she is really, you know, she used to be, *bigger*."

"Speaking of which," I say, "is this butter fat free?"

He smiles. "I haven't a clue."

"Why's she here? Do you know?"

"She's going with Sterling - for now."

"He never told me."

"Hell, he just told me yesterday."

I start looking around for napkins and a fork. I ask him where they are.

He hands me one fork and one napkin - they were on a table to the far right, next to an unopened bag of hot dog rolls (I don't see any hot dogs).

"You didn't make that, did you?" He points to the chili.

"What, are you kidding me?"

"Good."

There's a pause. I start to walk away but his voice makes me turn back. "Hey, did you hear what happened to Chris Giles?"

"Who?"

"Chris Giles - he played soccer with us, had that, dated that redhead Sylvie, that, she went to, oh I think it was Justice? Justice High?"

"Yeah, what about him?" I don't remember him at all.

"Annie heard from this friend of hers that went to college with him that in his junior year, he - get this - he hung himself at his fraternity over Christmas break when everyone was home and he stayed there alone. She thinks he had something like a 1.8 GPA, was on academic probation or something like that but no one knows if that's why he did it. That isn't the creepy part - the creepy part is that he was hanging there wearing nothing but a bow tie and black socks and boxers and left a note on his bedroom dresser that said 'Take eloquence and wring its neck.' Isn't that spooky?"

"Where did he hang himself?" I ask.

"Hmmm, uh, I think the railing."

"Would that hold him?"

"Beats me."

"Or the a light fixture? A fan?"

He just shrugs. "Man, I don't know."

"Was it in the local papers?"

"No idea. If it was, I missed it too."

"And how'd you say she found out?"

"A friend of hers that went to school with him. It was surrounded by speculation and hearsay and stuff like that. No one knows what really went on."

"I'm going to sit down someplace and eat these," I say, and start heading towards the corner of the yard far away from the steamer or Sterling or the sunbathers or pool hogs or volleyball players. I sit down on the grass, which feels like a shag carpet, Indian style, and slowly soak and torture the clam tissue in the cauldron of artery-clogging margarine.

Giles is but a vague whisper in my mind, and because high school seems so distant from me I find it hard to grasp

I'd even been there four years, gone, attended college, gone, worked and aged. I tossed my high school yearbook along with the journal I kept and maintained and got sick of. Frankly, I fail to find most of high school all that damn *relevant*, in hindsight (or perhaps its *relevance* exists in that it is a *precursor* of things to come). This sounds bitter, and such, but if I never hear of, or see, anyone I've heard of or seen for the last twenty five years of my walking and thinking, I don't believe it would be traumatic for me - it would be preferred.

A goofy brunette with large amber-tinted sunglasses that are a bit too large for her petite face is playing volleyball about 30 yards from where I am eating. Her body is fit and on the verge of being very toned - her abdomen is taut and her thighs streamlined. The bikini that's latched onto her flesh is a solid red (possibly off-red, perhaps magenta). I'm caught by the way she larks about, laughing with this other girl there (in a white T-shirt and Levi jean shorts), both having a grand-old time (or merely pretending to) trying to hit the elusive sphere that seems to bounce everywhere but in her favor, and both of them 'tag-teaming' to keep the ball airborne. Most of the time, though, it nails the ground, determined to invade their fists and palms. Their opponents on the other side of the net - two guys and one redhead (the two gentlemen not wearing T-shirts, only swimming trunks, sandals and wire-rimmed sunglasses; the redhead in a green tank top) appear genuinely amused by the Laurel and Hardy antics, and all five laugh and drink (in between points) from their clear cups which are boiling hot and resting on the side of the court. It's the sixth person - the French-toast-colored girl on the same team as the bumbling duo - that does not look at all amused - rather downright irritated - at how her 'team' was 'losing.' She randomly blurts out "Let's go" and "Ooooh!" very loudly, and runs around trying to be three people and make up for the ineptitude of the other two. I think, amidst the giggling and splashing (from the neighboring pool), I hear the irate third woman suggest that they 'Switch teams' or 'Just quit' or 'Just forget it,' but no one pays much attention to her.

Meanwhile, there's a lot of other things going on - small packs chat about work, kids, significant others, there are some folks tossing a foam pink-and-black football around, a good number are by the pool, either dipping their tootsies or relaxing or playing grab-ass in the deep end (the one girl, a pale brunette, is sitting on the shoulders of a mostly-submerged African-American man, who undoubtedly relishes her presence). All the while, I'm finishing up my dozen clams, and manually removing some salty bits from my tongue with the single napkin. That salt is the closest I've been to an ocean in forever.

"Devon!" I hear, to my left. It's Sterling, still topless, accompanied by the aforementioned Annie, not topless, both moving in my general direction from their corner of the yard to pester me.

"Why are you hiding over here?" Annie asks. I quickly rise to my feet, plate in hand.

"Oh-" Sterling opts to speak for me, "-he always does this. Remember in school? Always in the back of class, always causing trouble." She giggles.

"Trouble? I never caused any trouble," I fumble with the plate and set it back on the ground.

There's a pause and I guess I'm supposed to say something else with these two just looking at me blankly.

"So what's new with you, uh, Annie?"

"Not too much. Working. Going places."

"Sure, sure," I say.

Sterling turns to her and pretends to squeeze her head with his hands, making some loud *grrrr*-type noise. "You so tiny!" he emits.

"So what have you been up to?" she asks me, laughing and shooing away a playful Sterling.

"Not much. Work. You know."

"Yes I do."

"And I heard about what happened to Chris Giles. Davis just told me."

She shakes her head. "Isn't that *sad*? While I didn't let on when I was told the story, I swear I couldn't remember him. I had to peel through the yearbooks. And you know about the underpants and...."

"That's so - so out there," I say, "and frankly, I don't really remember him."

There's another extended pause. Neither of them says anything - Sterling seems to be transfixed by a blue jay/crow/robin redbreast swooping around the sky.

"So, are, uh, you guys an item?" I ask, breaking the silence.

She looks at Sterling who just shrugs. He says: "I guess." She says: "Sort of."

"If you get married, you have to promise not to invite me."

She pauses for an instant. "Not invite you, why?"

"I don't like weddings."

Playful mocking, on her part: "Do they make you cry?"

"No, it's not that."

"So you won't be getting married yourself."

"Never," I say.

"Why?" (Real mock-motherly, I think.)

I pause and try to come up with something good. "Because I believe I exist beyond sexuality."

"What?"

Sterling steps in. "What he means is that he likes playing with himself."

She laughs and covers her nose and mouth with her left hand (I laugh as well), and Sterling shrugs and then wraps his whole arm around her neck, as in a head-lock, and she laughs harder and then he starts to walk away, dragging her with him, and she's yelling combinations of "Let go," "Stop," and "Oww" as they make their way over to the liver-shaped swimming pool, which is full enough as is, and when they approach the rim he picks her up the way Tarzan would pick up Jane and dumps her, shaking and flailing all the way, into the deep end, bumping into the inflatable green sea horse. I'm still standing, plate of food on the ground, watching all of this, forgetting to move.

Since I don't want to sit outside anymore with the noise and the heat, I grab another dish of clams, butter and napkin from Davis, who has since had to change his T-shirt and apron, and proceed indoors, specifically the TV set room to consume the rest of lunch/dinner and leave as soon as I can, avoiding more awkward conversations between Sterling and Davis and anyone else. There are plenty of strangers wandering around the hardwood floors and cedar paneling of Marie's home, which, other than the TV room, is mostly sorted and clean and orderly. The kitchen, if anything, will require the most work when the day is done - already it has accumulated pots and pans and had tomato sauce spilled on its counter.

Once inside the vacant TV room I slide the couch closer to the entrance a couple of inches so I can slide between it and the wall and sit and eat my food and leave. I had contemplated taking the plate with me but I'm not too keen on infecting my car with the stubborn smell of seafood. I also figure - I might as well enjoy the central air-conditioning while I've got it - my apartment must be a furnace.

But I find that no, I cannot eat in peace and no, I cannot successfully hide as Marie, told by some mystery sniper concealed between the two glass statues in the living room must have spotted me in the TV room and ratted me out. The way she makes herself known is by tiptoeing by, slowly crawling on top of the couch and smacking me on top of the head (I'm busy looking down).

"I see you!" she tells me, as if I'm a child (which perhaps, oh, nevermind). "What are you doing down there?"

"How did you know I was here?"

"I watched you come in."

"Fantastic."

"When you leave, you *could* move the couch back."

"I know, I know. I'm sorry."

"So what's up? Davis said you weren't feeling well."

"Hmm?"

"He said you came in because you were sick."

I untwist myself and crawl out of the corner, standing, again with plate in hand. "I'm not sick - where'd he get that from?"

"I have no idea, that's what he told me."

"The food is really good," I tell her.

"I know. Your chili is really good."

"Thank you."

She slides over on the couch, tucks her legs underneath her. "Sit down. I want to talk to you." Her smile has gone away and her eyes have assumed a neutral position, focused and staring straight at me. She closes the door to the room with a swipe of her hand.

"Go on," she implores. I really want to leave, like, now, but *no*, I had to fucking eat more. I sit down, begrudgingly, with the plate in my lap.

She begins. "Now, I know your mother is handling Sterling's law suit."

"Uh-huh."

"What, oh, I don't know. What's going on with that?"

"With?"

"The *lawsuit*."

"I honestly have no idea. They never told me. I talked to her, she won't tell me."

"Yeah," she nods, "I thought so. Those two, actually, the three of them usually speak of it in hushed whispers and they all act suspicious and - look, I, I don't think of myself as a gossip or anything like that, but, you know, he just never *says* much of anything. About that or anything, really."

"He doesn't tell me anything either."

"We sit, at dinner, and nothing. He, I love him, but he, I mean, why can't he just be honest with me about, you know, it's like he's working for the government."

"But the case doesn't involve him, I think," I interject, finally comfortable enough to fork another clam into my mouth - sans butter.

"I know that, but he was there."

"Where?"

"At the party where it took place."

"So?"

"So, what was he doing there?"

"I wasn't there," I say.

"Where does he go when I'm not around?"

"Can't say."

"What does he do when you're with him?"

I pause. "We just drive and go out to eat. Where does he say we go?" I keep eyeing the door and hope this interrogation ends soon.

"He doesn't even say that. He usually just says, 'No place special.'"

"That's how guys are," I tell her, although I know she's read that about a dozen times in women's magazines, "it doesn't mean anything."

"But he was at a party when they were with those - kids."

"Maybe it was just once."

She looks at me with her chin down and eyes up in their sockets. "Oh *come on*."

"Why don't you just have a heart to heart with him?"

"Did you hear what I told you?"

"What do you want from me?"

She shrugs. "A little more."

"I don't know anything. He goes to parties, so what? He told me a long time ago you were fine with him going out with his friends."

"But he's *lying* to me now."

"Then kick him out."

She sighs and rubs her temples with her fingertips. "That's not what I mean."

"Then what do you mean?" I've finished all the clams.

She pulls her legs out from under her, folds them Indian-style.

"I feel like a fool," she tells me, and leans in. "A *complete fool.*"

"Oh *come on.*" I say. There's a pause. I take the plate and set it on the floor. She's still looking at me and I try to avert my eyes and pay a good deal of attention to the television set. I turn back to her and she's still looking at me.

"I'll tell you what," I concede, "- I'll see what I can find out."

"How?"

"I'll, I'll dig. I'll come up with something, and I'll send it to you or talk to you or something to that extent."

"You don't have to."

I scratch my ankle not because it's itchy or irritated but because I feel extremely agitated and need to move my hands. "You could have asked me this stuff on the phone the other day."

"*He* was around."

"Or beforehand? Like, months ago?"

"He's been acting stranger lately, saying less, never around."

"That's how he is, though."

"But I don't like it."

"Hey, you picked him."

She takes a while getting up but when she does she opens the door and wanders through the hallway and outside and chats with everyone again and even jumps in the pool, as calm and collected as if we never had this conversation.

I leave the plate on the floor and refuse to move the couch back and leave without saying goodbye to anyone.

Neutral.

a.) A while ago Sean came back to reclaim his cat, which I quickly took out of the box (along with its toy, the ball) and wiped up. In return, he brought me a decorative Mexican ornament comprised of dried red chilies that are somehow attached to each other. He told me he was going to hang his up in his kitchen, but I don't do that - I put it, on a hook, right above my bed so I have something to stare at before I doze off. He also asked if anyone came looking for him, and I said no, not that I knew of. He looked disappointed and trudged off.

b.) I turned in all of the paperwork (after making photocopies of everything, including the letters of recommendation, for future use) to Human Resources at the School District. She told me (the lady I handed it to, someone different than the last time I was in there) I'd be called for an interview in the "near future," which was too vague for my liking.

c.) I may not be able to completely convince you of this, and I'm not even sure how to say this, but ... in my head there is this ... *symphony* playing twentyfourseven, and my face doesn't show it but it's going full fucking tilt, like *Messiaen* at his most frenzied, all over the goddamn scale, all the goddamn time. Believe me. Believe me.

11.

Based on past experience and the ability to recall trivial pieces of dialogue and small scenarios I've experienced in my "life" (but inability to remember important ones, alas) I know exactly how I'm going to get into my Mom's law office, located on Chestnut Street, building #297, red brick.

Occasionally, I remember people - quite clearly, however these are odd occurrences. For example, the other day I sort of feigned knowledge of who Annie was. The truth is that yes I remember her, but no I did not want to make out that I did - how she would over-abuse lipstick so her mouth was whorish and bright, the obnoxious amounts of perfume that she sprayed on her various contact points, the nervous tick she had (but did not notice this time) where she would scratch her forearms with her razor-sharp fingernails producing bright pink jagged lines on them (as if she had been ravaged by a small woodland beast) and the baggy clothing she was fond of - sweatshirts, wide 'swish'-y jogging pants and the like. I do not recall how she treated Sterling or Davis but she was more or less indifferent towards me.

Giles, on the other hand, remains a dimly lit fragment in my mental Christmas tree. And I have no actual picture of him.

Despite all these forgettings-and-rememberings I do keenly recall something that will aid me on my quest, and it deals with my Mom's office building (she owns it, but there are two other tenants in there, one on the second floor, one on the third, each with their own clientele). Along with these floors, there's also this "basement level" (which isn't exactly a basement but let's not argue semantics ... or architecture) where she keeps most of her old files and also where her one secretary (Jean - in her 40's, rough, taut complexion, flat, uncombed mess of hair, unmarried) has a window by her desk that's been broken forever. My Mom, being the cheapie she is, has never been extremely concerned with getting it fixed (she gets sidetracked easily, sort of like Errol Flynn at a field hockey match) and (I pray, believe, hope) it remains broken to this very day. No, no, none of the windows are out or anything like that - poor, poor Jean would freeze in the wintertime - and it opens and closes fine, but it just doesn't lock. It *used* to lock, but do-it-yourself Jean turned herself into Bob Vila one sweltering summer afternoon and wisely used a hammer to pry open the "seemingly" jammed lock. It opened - presto - but with the lock mechanism completely scratched and in shambles. Mother commissioned father to take a look at it - with me along for the hell of it - and together we came to the brilliant conclusion that we couldn't do anything about it. This deduction took about three minutes to arrive at - how efficient!

So I figure this is my only real way in. Had I intended to do this before I would have gotten a key made for the main door or found some other way to pilfer the papers, but I can't *now*, so this is probably the only way, or the only way I care to think about and utilize. I asked kindly the first few times, the next one will not be so kind.

Quickly, about Marie: Nothing I find or read about (if anything) will be revealed to anyone, especially not her. I disapprove of the way she cornered me, and the way I felt "set up." Now I can wallow in the knowledge I do receive, and keep her in the dark. Masochistic? To some extent. An assault on her being overtly *forward*? This, my people, carries significantly more weight. She does deserve a tinge of credit for reminding me to do this, however. I've been planning it for forever and holding off and postponing the procedure.

Of course, there is an obstacle to this course, this *plan of action*: the alarm detector, which she does have installed (she didn't want it, but the other lawyers insisted) and the main panel of which is located to the right of the front door. But I am going in the basement! I basically figure out how the worst-case scenario - me being caught by the police - wouldn't really be *that bad*: Would my mother risk her reputation (and monthly rent payments from the other attorneys) by sending her son to jail for breaking and entering? She'd most likely construct some excuse for my presence, verbally brush the whole thing off and deal with me herself. And then what is she and father going to do? Hang me? Eloquent, I am not.

Of all the potential nights I could attempt this I try Wednesday because ... well, just because. I can only hope that her other secretary - Nancy, in her late 20's (possibly now 30's, now that I think about it) - isn't staying late to finish up paperwork, filing and such. I know Jean won't be there - she never stays after 5, and I'm pretty sure the other attorneys won't be. As for Mom, sometimes she goes country line dancing on Wednesdays with Dad. Picturing this in my mind has always produced a hysterical image, and I chuckle as my folks - two "Professionals" - try to 'get down' and behave as if they were born and raised in Tennessee. They see it as "good exercise" and "a lot of fun" and a chance to "get out of the house."

I arrived around 9:30 PM, after I finished slow sipping my decaffeinated green tea, got dressed and screwed my courage to the sticking place. My car, which is a black Honda Civic, blends nicely in with the unlit alleyway across the street which, although a little bit far to have to get to in a hurry, is completely unoccupied, so I don't have to worry about blocking it up (there's just enough room for two cars to get through side by side). I take proper dress precautions - black socks, baggy black sweatpants, black sweatshirt, black ski mask and black gloves (to conceal fingerprints), the latter two from my misadventures with Capo. I realize this is all very elaborate and borderline obnoxious (not to mention sweaty - it was something like 89° earlier today), but I kind-of like the feel of being a spy ... a very quixotic spy.

I had the thought ahead of time about the possible combination(s) for the alarm system - it has been '7135' for so long that I doubt if it was changed, but you never know. Ever since the one attorney left in a huff (over financial disputes and space requirements - what else?) she had meant to change it, but (to my knowledge) hasn't (I haven't been speaking to her that often or visiting for holidays so I don't keep up with her personal business and would never ask such *direct* questions to avoid suspicion).

There don't appear to be any lights on any of the floors as I'm seated in my car and waiting patiently outside, no strange activity, no cars outside, lying idle. The building next door, which is more of a beige-y tone (depends on the way the sun hits it - it can also appear cream-colored) and also contains a gaggle of lawyers, two of whom drive motorcycles (BMW, both bright red, both look like they're out of some sci-fi comic) to and from work. So what have we learned from this, kids? Lawyers either want to be cowboys dancing in the sand or leftovers from Hell's Angels. Is there an in-between?

Using the latest in stealth-like maneuvers, I sneak out of my car and gently press the door shut (to silence that gentle 'Ding-Ding-Ding' noise), tuck my car keys behind a bottle of Heineken lying in the alley way (which I've rested by the back right wheel), take a good look around to see if anyone else is in the alleyway (mine's the only car there, but it is far enough away from the main street and Mom's building to not make it look *too* out-of-place) and dart full speed across Chestnut Street, wisely avoiding the circular glow of the streetlights as they reflect on the still-warm asphalt. I could have walked casually, but considering the way I'm dressed (especially in August, of all months), it's the best way. I work my way around the front of the building, down the alley right next to it and around the dilapidated old garage that smells like cat piss and has two of its three windows completely broken, my guess by either errant baseballs or careless owners. It's only about 6 feet tall, a little higher vertically than I, and that's including the roof.

I swiftly move around this poorly painted, poorly maintained box through shrubs and small, withering trees that are in the backyard. You see, in this part of town, the buildings are all squashed together, and right behind the lawyer's office buildings are people's houses - facing in the opposite direction - with whom they share backyards and even grass. I'm sure there are established property boundaries, but these are pretty much ignored, as the home right behind my Mom's office decided - without asking - to plant a garden on both theirs and her property. It is this square land mass that I gleefully trample over on my way to the back windows, possibly killing someone's salad. Too bad.

The window in question is right next to a steel door that always stays locked and is never, ever, unlocked. I don't know who has the key to this (Mom must, obviously, but I wonder exactly who has it - does she even know?).

The window is shut, naturally, but low enough to the ground to easily get in and fairly wide to squeeze through (not that I'm fat - on the contrary, due to my calculated diet).

I have a hard time getting a firm grip on the window, and the soft gloves are impeding my progress. I reluctantly remove them, and place my palms on the window, emit a deep but barely audible "Ungh" (a War Cry for Mutes) and slide up the old-fashioned, chipped wood window, which does not have a screen behind it, luckily. I put my left leg in first and wave it around to get a good idea what I'm about to step on. I work the other leg, going in backwards and landing with both feet on hardwood floor. I decide to leave the window ajar for my escape, and I can only hope that no one wanders into his or her backyard with a hankering for tomatoes.

It is at this point that I come to the realization that I have forgotten a very valuable item and violated a commonly held rule for thieves: bring a flashlight. With it, you can *see* in the *dark*, which would be useful right about now. However, the flashlight does have its drawbacks, and, should someone outside see it, a la Watergate, they know something's amiss. I could play it cool and turn on the lights, but opt not to and risk shuffling around aimlessly in the dark and risk bruises and knocking over things and black and blue marks.

I gain footing and orient myself so I know where Jean's desk is, then shuffle around the corner. I don't remember where the alarm sensor is so I bolt down the basement hallway and up the steps as fast as I humanly can, and the minute I set foot on the steps to proceed to floor one, I hear it:

BEEP

BEEP

I run up the steps, stumbling but not falling over one of the middle ones, to the first floor, then down another hall towards the front door where the alarm system is situated nearby. The streetlight is now a welcome assistant, and with its glowing radiance filtering through the front window I can make out the buttons on the keypad.

7-1-3-5

BEEP

I try again: 7-1-3-5

BEEP

Frantic, I input the digits very slowly, taking extra time to push in each individual button very carefully, forcefully, so the rubber plastic squares with numbers on them go as far back as they possibly can, and then some.

7-1-3-5

BEEP

A sudden flush forms in my cheeks and runs down the back of my neck as I realize she changed it - or the Security Systems people did, for that matter, and so I start pounding in random digits, for birthdays: hers, 0-4-2-1, BEEP, Dad's, 0-7-0-6, BEEP, mine, 1-2-1-5, BEEP. Nothing.

Unable to think of much else, and realizing that the authorities/unwanted attention may gather by soon, with the incessant beeping and all (PoPo HQ becomes notified after a set period of time of the alarm having gone off, after which the hive sends out the guard bees to take care of business). Figuring I have a good five minutes, I immediately make for Mom's office, where she keeps most of the recent cases. I turn on the room lights and look at the stack of manila folders, all labeled by last name, first name (they are all alphabetical). Not there. I scavenge the piles around and on top of her desk. Nothing, only notes and random pieces of paper and family pictures. I then go to the three filing cabinets, all in a row in the other room, nine drawers in all, each drawer containing a part of the alphabet. I find "G-H-I," first cabinet, third drawer down, open it, and leaf through for "Harrison." "Hall," "Harner," boom. "Harrison, Sterling." I grab the folder, close the door and turn off the lights. I can't tell if there are sirens going outside because of the constant BEEPing irritating my head, which is the digital equivalent of someone standing outside and screaming "Criminal!" as loud as their organs will allow.

I make like a long distance runner and bolt down the steps to the basement, down the hallway, my heart pounding pounding pounding and my vision blurred by pulsing veins and bright white dots, and before I get to the open window I run right into the corner of Jean's desk, which must double as a medieval torture device, its edges like spears digging into my left calf. I withhold an angry, pain-infused obscenity and drop the folder but manage to look past the pain and scramble for the papers and get back on my feet, go out the window head first, my hands touching the ground, and wiggle out the rest of my person and slide the window shut, muffling the harsh BEEPs but not silencing them entirely.

I turn and fly down the alleyway, manila packet in right hand. I could swear there's life stirring in the neighborhood, and as I dash past several houses I could swear I hear people ruminating and mumbling on their patios and balconies, from inside their kitchens and bedrooms. I run and run and run (or rather, hobble hobble hobble, with my left leg emitting a sharp pain with every step) down so many streets that I lose track of where I am, them turn left by some bushes in someone's backyard and just dive in, being poked and scratched at by branches, prickly points jabbing me from every direction. The ends of the bushes keep getting in my eyes, but I only fidget gently to move them - I don't want to make too much noise. The way I see it, I'm not sure anyone will see me in the bushes, it's far too dark (and I don't see any lights on in the houses around me). Likewise, I can't see out of the brush, with leaves and twigs blocking out most everything.

I wait for an exaggerated period of time in here - eventually, I grow desensitized to the foliage surrounding me the way one of those *people* learn to deal with lying on a bed of sharp nails (aren't they Buddhists? or am I thinking of some other religion?). I don't bother to lift my head to hear, I just rely on my ears and ears alone. Not once while in here have I heard (a.) sirens or (b.) the Security System or (c.) conversations being held close by.

I keep thinking I ran over three or four blocks away, but it's clearly hard to tell.

I creep out of the area I was in, casually brush off the stubborn pieces of plant that don't want to see me leave, roll up my sweatpants and the sleeves on my sweatshirt (which is a welcome relief - I am sweating profusely) and take off my ski mask and stuff that into my pocket. I inconspicuously head up the road I came from, acting like I belong, trying to walk off my sore leg (which I was massaging with my fingertips) and treating my journey to the car like a casual night walk some people naively take in Central Park. The manila folder, though wickedly crinkled, is still rolled up in my right hand. I fail to spot any activity in the surrounding neighborhood, no talking, no TV sets playing.

As I near the side of Mom's building, something strikes me: no one is around. Not a single person. The lights on all the floors of the building are still off. There's no cars in the street in front, no cops, no Mom or Dad (perhaps they're somewhere they can't be reached). If there's BEEPing, I can't hear it.

I walk over to my car, my eyes dodging left and right, waiting for people to spring up on me, but I don't spot anything I might interpret as suspicious. I go over to the Heineken bottle and move it and pick up my keys.

As I get in and sit down, I look back at the building and now worry about Step 2: getting the damn thing back in. Call it the sequel.

I start the car and drive over to the FastStop where I make photocopies of the folder's contents (for 5¢ a copy). Before I enter, however, I make sure to tear off the black sweatshirt I had on, with just my plain white T-shirt on underneath, and my sweatpants still rolled up. I don't intend on acting suspicious. They might think I'm trying to rob *this place* too.

The photocopies come to $2.05 for all 41 pages. I made copies of absolutely every piece of nonsense in there, from facts and figures to faxes and letters and memos Mom wrote to Nancy to photocopies of precedent cases out of hard-bound law texts to information that has a World Wide Web address on it and came off the Internet.

I also spend $10 on a flashlight and $4 on 2 D batteries. The thin, gaunt kid who rings up my order didn't find my legal photocopies or flashlight purchase suspicious at all - frankly, he just looked tired.

Step 2 is mostly brain-dead because I not only have any real logical means of re-entry - to return the manila folder - but because I don't have time to dawdle and figure out some brilliant way of putting back the papers.

However, Step 2 will be a little better constructed than Step 1. This time, I will not park the car anywhere near the office. Rather, I will park it down three streets, near where I was in the bushes. I will proceed in the same way, through the window, up the stairs, straight to the filing cabinet (no more turning on light switches), bypassing superfluous, time-wasting tinkering with the Security System. After returning the file I run again, hide in the bushes (again, yes, this is redundant), motionless, wait for a period of time, get inside the car, drive away, shower. Not simple - clunky, as a matter of fact.

I park the car on York Street, which is a block down from where the bushes are. It would be nice if I had an accomplice to man the vehicle, but I figure it's best to do this alone. After rolling down the sweatpants and putting on the sweatshirt (I'm carrying the ski mask and will put it on the closer I get to the building), and putting the keys by the back wheel (although no garbage or bottles are around to cover it with), I take the folder and flashlight (which I already put the batteries in) and go for a stroll. I pass several windows in nearby homes: in one, a young man is eating cookies in his kitchen while reading a magazine (can't tell which one), in another, there are a dozen lights on in one room - lamps of all sorts - but the television is on and there's no one around. There are newspaper pages spread about all over the floor, covering everything. Perhaps this resident (or residents) is toilet training a new home companion (dog, cat, exotic animal) or painting something (the ceiling, possibly) or (c.) none of the above.

As I near the building, I put on the ski mask, tuck the manila folder in my pants, keep the flashlight in my right hand and repeat the last procedure, around the broken down garage/shed, tiptoe around the vegetable garden, towards the window, slide it back up, and crawl in, get inside, stay down low. I turn on the flashlight so I don't run into any desks again and dart up the steps again, triggering the troubling BEEPing once again. I waste no time and make a b-line for the filing cabinets, finding "Harner" again, sliding the crinkled and abused folder out of my shirt/pants, carefully placing it back in the drawer, closing it and, with the flashlight leading the way, go through the first floor hallway, the stairs, another hallway and past Jean's desk and out the window yet again. When I do get outside I set the flashlight on the ground so I can use both hands to close the window, I notice that the light is shining on two familiar objects that link me to this: the black gloves, which I initially took off upon Step 1's entry. Apparently the Police Officers - if they were the ones who turned off the alarm the first time - never saw them.

I push down the window to ensure it is completely shut, and then use one of the gloves to wipe away fingerprints on the windowpane that could implicate me, grab my things and make down the street again, not quite so nervous as last - since I made record time with this trial - but still hustling nonetheless. I arrive at the same bundle of bushes, dive back in and get reacquainted with my prickly cohorts. My heart is pounding from the run - an easy 130/140 beats per minute - and I continue to perspire (my lower back could easily fill an 8-oz jar - my T-shirt is stuck on my skin). Salty sweat makes its way towards my eyes, past my ineffective eyebrows, producing stinging and burning, and I wipe at them with my gloved hand, hoping to absorb some of the liquid and ease the pain. My thigh is still sore from the earlier incident.

It is unfortunate that I never brought a watch with me, as it would have been convenient to know how long I've laid here, twisted, like a contortionist. Perhaps it is best to operate instinctually in scenarios like these, relying on sense rather than time.

After waiting and thinking, and engaging in some basic form of "mindfulness" Buddhists speak of (involving counting breaths, inhale, one, exhale, two, inhale, three, exhale, four, *and so on*), I arise out of the bushes, and look down the road. I can't make out much but I think I see a flickering blue light and hear some human voices coming from someplace. I remove the mask, pace suspiciously to the black Honda, not bothering to wipe myself free of leaves and bristles and twig fragments, and start the car.

As I drive away I look left and see and older man and woman standing outside the door of their home, staring right at me. The old woman turns and says something to her significant other and I step on the gas and drive away. What did she say? Was it about me? Was that a blue light down there from a police car or the aural glow off a television set? I keep one eye behind me, in the rear-view, trying to see if anyone is behind me. I don't see anyone.

I drive home very slowly, keeping an eye out for anything. I try to keep the speedometer someplace between too slow and too fast - around 35 or 40.

But precautions and cautious driving, I feel, are a waste of time. Fate has, perhaps, a better say (though blaming fate is, alas, a lame character flaw) and as I make my way down Pacific Avenue, on my way to the bridge that takes me over to the other side of town and home, blue and red flashing lights flicker and loud sirens blare behind me, out of absolutely nowhere (though I must admit I hadn't been paying much attention to the rear-view for the past few miles). Startled once again, my heart resumes its pounding, its thumping reverberating in my ears and eyes. I pull over, put the car in park, place my hands on the steering wheel and tilt my head back. When I look in the rearview, I notice the two Police Officers are still seated there, looking down, (I think) saying something to each other. I take this opportunity to cover up some things so I take the flashlight and the photocopies and the ski mask and stuff them under the seat (I had contemplated using this break to drive away, but that would only make more problems). I just sit and wait for the eminent arrival of my sentence.

The figure coming near me is a dark-skinned Police Officer with his own flashlight, which he shines on both me and the rest of the insides of the car. He leans over.

I'm deep breathing, gasping for air, and try to beat him to the punch. "Sir, you see, I had...."

But his voice stops me from talking. "Could you give me your driver's license and car registration?"

I fumble with the contents of the glove compartment, which I asked if I could go through and he said "Sure" to. I find it in there, along with my wallet (where I obviously keep my driver's license), and hand both to him.

"Stay here," he tells me. He walks away with both items. I don't plan on leaving.

Cars passing by appear to slow down and gawk at the guy being pulled over, and all I can do is try to cover the left side of my face with my left hand.

The sweat continues to pour down my lower back, and face, and upper trunk, and forehead. The car must reek of it by now even though the driver's side window is down. I keep glancing in my rearview to see what's going on, or when the other one is going to step out and lend some assistance, but that doesn't happen. The same one gets out again, and makes his way back over to me.

He hands me three things: the license, registration and a mysterious third paper.

"Back there you missed a Stop sign," he tells me.

"I did what?"

He repeats himself (as I'm sure he's used to), and then I tell him I just didn't see it, that it must have been hidden in foliage, and that I'm deeply sorry, and that has never ever happened before, and he tells me some other things I don't care about but I keep nodding anyway. He walks away and I say "Thank you" and "Sorry about all this" but I'm not sure he hears me or if he does, doesn't say anything in return.

My blood pressure and heart valves breathe a monstrous sigh of relief.

They let me leave first, and I do, very slowly and very carefully, and I putter over the bridge and back to my apartment, with all of the car's four windows down. If I kept any sort of alcohol or drug in the apartment, now is the time I would use them, but since I don't, I'll settle on a shower.

To think: *this could all have been averted if....*

12.

The fine for the entire Stop sign ordeal is $93.50, which I could protest with a lawyer, but I figure it's not that much and write the check and mail it in. I figure: at least I'm helping them fund whatever highway they decide to revamp.

I skip work today to recoup and rub ice on my sore leg, which probably doesn't need it, though I feel bored and need to do something, and examine the photocopies with the utmost care, precision and accuracy.

Disappointingly, a lot of what is in the mimeographed documents is too jargon-laden and insignificant to make much sense. I therefore go through the process of sifting out the nonsense to find understandable information. Precedents, letters from another lawyer - Mr. Raymond Dirk - to Mom, letters from Mom to the court, letters from Mom to the client (Sterling), memos to Nancy, one memo to Jean, one memo reminding her to tell Sterling something (I think - it's made of initials and broken word fragments and looks more like a word jumble than anything substantial), a letter from Mom to some other attorney (a Mr. Jackson Cooper), etc. I recall when reading past documents Mom would have lying around I would see a "transcript"-type packet lying around, typed by either a magistrate or court stenographer or neither, which read basically like some stage play, with all the syntax being 'Name' ':' '<statement>' for each person. But nothing of the sort is in what I photocopied, and I am truly disappointed.

One of the only segments of relevant information provides a skeleton for my personal understanding, and gives me a foundation as to what may or may not have gone on. The following is essentially edited, for you, with only what I deem the relevant parts included (had I included the whole thing - *gasp* - I'd develop CTS).

The total page count in the original is fifteen pages. Here's an excerpt, with lapses or intentional breaks indicated by a "..." and relevant dates and numbers and the like removed. I also edited it for your convenience:

ELIZABETH STRIDE, *minor*, by)
NATHANIEL STRIDE, and)
JESSICA STRIDE, H/W, individually)
and as parents of the minor,)
          Plaintiffs,) No. __-__-__
    vs.) Jury Trial
STERLING HARRISON,) Demanded
         Defendant)

COMPLAINT

COME NOW, Plaintiffs, Elizabeth Stride, a minor, by and through Nathaniel Stride and Jessica Stride, husband and wife, individually and as her parents, by and through their legal counsel, COOPER & DUGREY, LAW OFFICES, P.C. and over as follows:

...

IV. FACTUAL MATTERS

8. On or about _____, in the late evening, Plaintiff Elizabeth Stride, hereinafter referred to as Plaintiff, Defendant Harrison, hereinafter referred to as Defendant, and many other individuals (approximately 30), including Dawn Fields, Davis Klein, Eric Blair and Avrane Oman were at a party on Glendon Drive, home owned by the parents of Janelle Fisk.

9. While at the Glendon Drive home Plaintiff, located in the downstairs living room, along with friends Dawn Fields and Avrane Oman, saw Defendant, who arrived with Davis Klein and Eric Blair, came over and asked Plaintiff to come outside with him to talk.

10. Plaintiff agreed and followed Defendant out the back door.

11. While outside Defendant asked Plaintiff if she wanted to leave the party. Plaintiff told him "No."

12. Defendant then asked Plaintiff to accompany him to a room upstairs to be "more alone." Plaintiff complied.

13. Upon going upstairs, Defendant asked Plaintiff into the bedroom of Janelle Fisk's parents, who own the home, which, at that time, was the only room vacant.

14. Plaintiff and Defendant were both in the room, with Plaintiff sitting on a chair and Defendant on the bed. They spoke for some time.

15. Defendant eventually got up to close the door to the room, as the outside music and talking were becoming disruptive.

16. Defendant locked the door, against Plaintiff's request to leave it unlocked.

17. Defendant then proceeded to move closer to Plaintiff, who was becoming nervous and frightened. She asked him to cease moving closer. He refused.

18. After some conversation, Defendant grabbed Plaintiff by the hair and proceeded to try to kiss her on the mouth and fondle her breasts through the sweater she was wearing.

19. Plaintiff struggled to free herself from Defendant's grasp but he was too strong. He picked her up by the hair and pushed her against the wall and began licking her neck, while pinning both of her arms against the bedroom wall.

20. Plaintiff, frightened, began to yell for help, but the outside noise coming from the living room made it hard to hear.

21. Defendant released her arms and began pulling off Plaintiff's sweater. Plaintiff fought but, again, Defendant was too strong and succeeded in getting the sweater off.

22. Next, Defendant began to remove Plaintiff's jeans.

23. Plaintiff tried to get towards the bedroom door to unlock it and escape, all the while hollering for help, but Defendant grabbed her hair and dragged her to the ground.

24. Defendant then proceeded to remove her jeans. Plaintiff, at this point in fear for her life, complied with Defendant's request to turn over onto her back.

25. After doing so, Defendant removed his pants and forced Plaintiff's legs apart, penetrating her vagina with his penis. Startled and scared, she continued struggling and demanded he stop at once. He refused.

26. While penetrating her on the floor, Defendant Harrison had forced his hand into Plaintiff Stride's mouth, causing her to gag and have difficulty breathing. Several times Plaintiff Stride tried to get away, but Defendant Harrison's strength kept overpowering her. She tried biting his hand, but this did not stop the attack.

27. After Defendant Harrison had finished he pulled up his pants and exited the bedroom, leaving Plaintiff Stride on the bedroom floor.

28. Plaintiff Stride put her clothing back on and waited a period of time so she could stop crying. She was embarrassed and frightened and did not want her friends to see her in such a condition.

29. When she left the room, Plaintiff Stride located her friends Avrane Oman and Dawn Fields and asked to leave.

30. Upon arriving home, Mrs. Stride noticed something was wrong with Plaintiff Stride. Plaintiff Stride continued to describe the incident to her mother.

...

44. ... Defendant Hamilton entered a nolo contendere plea to Statutory Sexual Assault and Corruption of Minors in the Criminal Division....

... Etc, etc.

After that there is this "CLAIMS" part that has several "Counts" and various other legalese, law jargon and the like scrawled in there. In summation, Count 1 is for "Assault," and the Plaintiffs' request "Three Million Dollars," plus "costs, interest and other relief this Honorable Court may deem appropriate and necessary." Count II is for "Battery," which lists various injuries this girl sustained, including "insomnia," "medical expenses," "loss of wages," "humiliation and shock," "sexual dysfunction," "loss of self-esteem and self-worth," "loss of reputation in the area," and more. For this they request four million. Count III is for "Intentional Infliction of Emotional Distress," which does state that the Plaintiff endured "humiliation," "embarrassment," and "psychological trauma" (among others), continues to suffer, and requires counseling, psychological treatment, has suffered a "loss of enjoyment of life," and about a dozen other things. This comes to another four million. The last count (yes, there is more) is for "Negligent Infliction of Emotional Distress." It essentially repeats the last caption and says how careless Sterling was in acting the way he did. Once again, the bill for this one is four million.

All in all, the total requested price tag is something like fifteen million dollars. Add five more and you could hire Tom Hanks to narrate the TV movie. In all seriousness, though, this is an astonishing amount of money. Since the Complaint is only the girl's side of the story - not Sterling's - I can't say how accurate it is (his story will probably be radically different). I don't know how "relaxed" he'll be when he has to pay some (if not all) of this money back - it's impossible for him to do so (I guess insurance picks it up - I was never apt to pay much attention to Mom discussing law). Considering the fact that I've known this guy for so long - ten plus years - and used to discuss hockey and sports in the lunch room and gossip quietly about others, you'd think I'd say that "Oh, he would never do that." While I'm inclined to, I will not. Frankly, I don't think there's anything anybody *won't* do, him included. I wouldn't put this past Davis either. Not that they aren't half-decent people - they aren't great, they aren't horrible - and call me pessimistic, but these things do happen, unfortunate as they may be. And they always will happen, sad to say.

More thinking produces more questions, but there's a lot the document didn't say. How old was this girl, by the way? What was the average age of the people at this party? Since when do younger girls invite older guys to such events? Oh, the last one reveals my naiveté, I think.

Either way, I am partially grateful I did not go with them that particular night, as I would not be amused to find my name listed in *any* document of that sort. My father always warned me - as every single father is programmed to do - not to associate with people of questionable character. This goes to show you I'm not the best when it comes to following directions, orders and taking advice.

13.

Surprisingly, Mom has not called, suspecting me of being a Hoodlum and a Criminal, nor have the Police come breaking my door down (I slid one of my many wood dressers in front of it just in case). Perhaps ... and this is a *perhaps* ... perhaps I did such a fantastic job, I left zero trace of my presence! Perhaps I missed my true calling as a Professional Kleptomaniac/Thief-For-Hire.

And yes, my leg is feeling better - thank you for thinking of me.

I was phoned the other day by the School District for an interview in the Human Resources Department, and the "Head" of Human Resources. I scheduled it for 3 PM on Tuesday - how ordinary - and will simply leave work early to make it.

———

The Human Resources Office is just as clean and orderly as it was the last two times I was here, which suggests, or shows a significant result, that the office is consistently clean and orderly, not simply a fluke the first time I entered.

There's a strange/pungent scent of Italian (or Caesar?) Salad Dressing - all those naughty herbs and spices - lingering in the air. The strong vinegar-ish smell reminds me of the unwanted reek of body odor, but it isn't quite so potent that you feel completely suffocated or anything like that - only mildly bothers me. There are windows in this office that (I think) can be opened, but none seem to be.

I basically stand in the entranceway by the Secretary's pavilion to wait for my Interviewer to escort me to someplace more private. The Secretary made a call to someone as soon as I arrived, and took my name, but it's been a while and no one has come by. I begin fidgeting, taking my hands in and out of my pockets, shifting weight from one leg to the other, playing uncomfortably with my shirt collar and neck tie, which is more like a hangman's noose than a fashion accessory for the moment.

As soon as I start peeking my head around walls and into rooms nearby the Secretary catches my 'restlessness' in the corner of her eye and reassures me that, "They'll be just a minute." They could have a chair or a stool or a beanbag chair for me to sit in. It's not like I'm waiting in line at a restaurant to enjoy a meal - I'm going to be carted off to a room filled with other people who are being paid to judge me.

Some time later a thin, odd-looking blonde woman with a mouth that doesn't seem to align properly (her lower jaw hooks to the left slightly, and her smile reveals more teeth than a normal person usually has) as well as a lopsided hairdo - all the hair goes from right to left, leaving the left side with only a sparse amount covering it, as if a giant fan had sent a torrent of wind from over her right shoulder. Combined, it's almost as if her head is being pulled in two completely opposite directions at once, East and West. I pray the expression on my face when we met wasn't one of bewilderment. I would be saddened should someone ever look at me in such a way.

I follow this woman to an office down one of the corridors, down to the right. Inside the door she leads me to the 'interviewing area.' There are five objects in the room in total: a table and four metallic chairs (one at the one side, three on the other). She points me to the chair I am to sit at - the single - and instructs me to be patient and wait, while she quickly works her way out of the area to either fetch the appropriate personnel or do some other job-related errand or (potentially) use the toilet. Before she goes she closes the door behind her, as if at the last minute I might try to make a run for it.

A minute later I hear rustling outside and the door opens and three people - two women and a man - come in to greet me, already engaged in some sort of discussion amongst themselves, of which I only hear the last few vowels and consonants before they all laugh simultaneously, right on cue. After the laugh that conversation ends and they take the attention off each other and place it right on me. Each of them offers me a greeting and a handshake, which I stand up and reluctantly accept, starting with the man, who sits in the center seat opposite me (he's Mr. Saul, the Chief Coordinator of Human Resources - a chubby fellow with a huge black pompadour). His hand is warmer to the touch as compared to Heather's, who sits to his right (and my left). Heather is the Assistant Coordinator of Human Resources, and, like the woman who brought me into this room, possesses bleached-blonde hair, but unlike that other woman, parts her hair 50/50, half right and half left, and no discernable jaw problem. She also looks sewn into the purple one-piece she's wearing, which sucks to her skin like Saran Wrap and accents the unpleasant paunch around her midsection.

Hannah is the second female (seated to Mr. Saul's left, my right) and, once again, is bleached blonde, slightly saggy under the chin and cheeks, and seemingly more reserved in terms of attire. When I shake her hand she only tells me her first name and it takes the on-the-ball Mr. Saul to fill in that she's Heather's Assistant (which would, consequently, make her the Assistant to the Assistant Coordinator of Human Resources, a title 50 letters or 57 characters long). I wonder how much she gets dumped on by her other colleagues.

Mr. Saul turns out to be the quarterback of this whole interview, while his two blonde, late 30, early 40-something Assistants shift their gazes from me, then to the blank pieces of paper they each have in front of them to scribble every phoneme I mumble on, then to each other, usually in that order. They don't say much of anything, laugh if there's a light moment, or ask any questions. I have no idea why both of them were dragged in here to do transcription - wouldn't one suffice? Or are they convinced that they can piece apart my answers to their inane questions better and come to a fuller understanding of *who I am* if they proceed in such a thorough fashion?

"So," Mr. Saul says, "You're interested in this Substitute position?"

"Yes," is all I reply, hands on lap.

"And ... well, tell us a little about you. What kind of person you are. Don't be shy." His hands are folded on top of the table and he's looking straight at me with a teensy smile.

"Well - I'm, I'm really just looking forward to a position that will challenge me and maybe teach me something about, um, teaching."

"Why do you want to do this? There are other jobs out there."

Damn it. "Like I said, it's challenging and hopefully fun and not at a desk where I was and I guess there's a bit of pride involved. Pride to help younger people."

He nods.

I continue, warily. "I remember, see - when I, I remember when I was in class, which wasn't too long ago, and I had teachers who, you know, you feel they don't handle things well or aren't understanding. I just wanted - to, uh, use that to, not do that same thing over again."

He glances over to the paper Heather is frantically scrawling on, then starts up again. "Tell me about your college experiences, if you remember them."

I wait a bit, causing Heather and Hannah to look up at me along with Mr. Saul, giving both of them a temporary reprieve from their dictation. "You mean-?"

"Well, teachers, classes, what you liked. Sports you played."

"I never played sports, there or in high school. I like ice hockey, though I don't have the patience to learn to skate. Don't like falling." I laugh, no one else does. "But classes and teachers were fine, in, college."

"What did you learn in some of your classes?"

"Which ones?"

"Pick one."

"I took a class in Child Psychology. I guess that's relevant to this."

"Right. What else was interesting to you?"

"I liked Photography. That was fun. And, well, so was Sociology and Group Dynamics."

Mr. Saul adjusts his shirt by pulling on his left sleeve. "Okay. What did you do in the-" he looks at Hannah's paper, "-in the Group Dynamics class?"

"We got into groups and had to-"

"What kinds of groups?"

"Teams. They divided the class into teams of, I think five or six. Then you picked a leader and worked on an assigned project."

"What did your group do?"

"Honestly I don't recall."

"Who was the leader?"

"Of our group?"

He shakes his head.

"The one girl. Anyway-"

"Why weren't you?"

See. What is this? I retort promptly. "You fail to understand how the class went. The teacher assigned groups, topics and leaders. I had no say in who did what. I simply did my best to do what was required of me."

"What about-," he looks to Heather's paper this time. Photography. Why that?"

"I liked being outdoors. It fascinated me, temporarily."

"What other activities were you involved in?"

I quickly scramble, searching for something. I think of what Davis did while at his school, and use that: "Fencing and Aikido. But mostly Aikido. It was relaxing for me."

"Aikido, huh? Lots of kicking and punching."

"No. It's a passive form of self-defense."

"I see."

More questions follow, the two blondes filled up both front and back of their once-blank paper, and needed to get more. There's an air-conditioning vent right above my head (which could be Item #6 in the room if you want to be picky) that blows in timed spurts right on my head, causing me to be chilled and develop a minute headache. That's why the windows weren't opened in the main office to ventilate the premises - the beauty of unregulated central air.

He is handed a piece of paper by Hannah, which was not hand-written, but made by a computer printer. "Now all I need you to do is answer these to the best of your ability. Okay?"

"Yes."

"What is your current position?"

I pause. "I'm an Administrative Technological Consultant."

"Okay, what does that mean?"

"Computer maintenance, customer interaction, insurance claims, lots of troubleshooting." Lie, lie, truth, lie.

"How many people do you work with at this job?"

I lie, again. "Five, mostly."

"Can you think of any recent event that took place where you needed to act quickly to resolve a problem? It could be anything."

The vent tosses icicles at me full-blast, causing the slight numbing pain on the top of my skull to inch up on the intensity scale. My hair, bushy as it is, offers little cover. I appear to be the only one in the room bothered by it.

I break out scenarios from novels to fill this in - it's better than nothing or saying 'And this matters *because*...?' "I can clearly recall one instance where the, um, Floor Manager and his Assistant needed our team - we were the, Blue Team, wait I'm jumping the gun. We had to fill out this major, let's just call it a report. Anyway, to make matters worse, Jenny, who was on our team, had a Dentist's appointment, so I stepped in and did my work, and hers, and I was there until about 8 PM doing everything, and the paper had to be done like, the day before, and we all scrambled and hustled until it was finished and set off that night for next morning. None of us got paid overtime or anything like that, but it was worth it, you know, it felt good - a relief."

"What did Jenny say?"

"Hmm?"

"The girl you covered for?"

"Oh, she bought us all donuts and coffee the next day. She was ecstatic. For Christmas she gave me a gift certificate to a restaurant."

"Good." He looks down at the paper again. The duo continue writing and not looking at me or him. "Now, what would you say your positive qualities are?"

"Well, I'm dependable, determined, dynamic, devoted, and, uh ... any other d-word you can think of." I smile a fake plastic smile, they do not. Hannah may be having trouble spelling "dynamic."

Following that are more questions - far too many for a part-time (!) position. Following that are more lies, more cold air. Shit, I wish I'd remembered to bring a watch. Damn, I wish I ate lunch today.

Mr. Saul rests his head in his right hand, palm up, scanning the sheet of paper with the appropriate-questions-to-ask-potential-employees. "And if you'd speak on behalf of someone else, who was asked to name your faults, what would they be?"

"Well," I think. I could name a dozen that would pretty much render me ineligible for this position, so I select words cautiously. "Sir, don't you think we all have a multitude of faults that we possess and wished we didn't? For every good, there is something that needs to be worked on. And to admit faults is to become a victim *of* those faults. So there I deny any glaring faults, and can only hope to do my all in any endeavors." I want to laugh, and break up, but I do not, I retain composure. None of them are laughing - what are *they* thinking?

"Okay," is all I get in response, no applause, no stale fruit tossed at me.

There are more questions still that I continue to blow off, this segment of the day has truly worn me down, it feels like forty some minutes have elapsed and I need to lie down to get rid of this headache. For these answers I mostly make up tall-tales. All the while I find that I can't tell much from their non-descriptive faces - am I a hit? -am I a disaster? This trio would be a nightmare to play cards with, which is misleading considering the state-of-merriment they appeared to be in before this interview took place.

He and his associates thank me for my time, which they wasted, and wish me good luck. I rise, shake hands (again) reluctantly (again) and follow them out to a much-warmer hallway. As a postscript Mr. Saul tells me that they will call me after they've decided whether or not I'd be "suitable" for the position, and if so, when the training session will be.

"Training Session?" I ask.

"We won't let you go in there cold," he says. "They tell you the basics, give you a head start."

"I see."

"There will be three other people with you in there for the same position, so you won't be alone."

"Oh, I thought there was just one opening."

"No, no. Don't worry about it, though - all teaching is hard at first until you get used to it. You'll adjust."

I think that is the hundredth time I've heard a statement of that nature delivered by a person experienced in a field to a person inexperienced - no one seems to say much different.

"I'm not concerned," I say.

I called the Church in regards to that position they advertised for as soon as I got home. An older woman answered.

It was filled two weeks ago.

14.

Either I'm a brilliant liar or they're ragingly desperate, because I got the phone call, at home, a week later, saying they want me for the Substitute Teaching position. This came to me with mixed sensations of relief and total dread - relief in change, dread in change. It's not like I want the job - hell, I'd rather not have any job - but when I feel anxious, I need to change immediately. There is no waiting. There is no negotiating with myself over myself. I always win.

I was notified that I'd have to attend a three-day seminar in the School District Headquarters (same place as last, and the time before, and the time before), come September 2nd. I was told it would last from 8 AM to 3 PM, normal school hours, in room 236, a normal-sized classroom.

Marie also phoned me sometime between now and then (a precise date eludes me, which I find frustrating, as always). She prodded and poked and chastised me for not following up on my initial goal (I lied and told her I opted not to be so crude - a sweet little lie). She was in a garrulous mood at the time (she did mention how I forgot to take home the Tupperware container I brought) and I wanted to get her off the phone, so I shifted the conversation from Davis (who wasn't home) and 'what I think of Z,' 'Z' being some personality quirk of his she decided on bringing up but I couldn't give a shit about - nonetheless two shits - and blindside her with questions regarding *Eros and Civilization* and its on-going relevance in contemporary America and she wondered what I was talking about but eventually got the message and the phone 'conversation' ceased to be. I just picked that book because it was on a shelf close to me while we spoke - I don't think I ever read it.

In preparation for starting this new position I began the process - at work - of cleaning out my desk. I tore down the poster of France, tossed it in the waste basket and took the fern and relocated it to one of the other dozens of vacant desks encircling mine, specifically one not close to me, down a ways. I placed it there with a toothpick embedded in the soil and this coquettish little note:

> Sweet gentleness
> and purity
> are all I can endure

I hope the individual - male or female - could use its company.

I also removed the contents of my desk drawers, magazine clippings (with one on "How to Build a Birdhouse" that I planned on following up on but never have), random pens, my sketch pad, dull steel scissors (that irritate your thumb and index finger with its rusty steel frame) as well as a photograph of me, in my collegiate cap and gown, tired and distracted, with the word "subvert" emblazoned (in white-out) on the roof of the cap. All objects were thrown, the picture shredded.

Since I can't find anyone to report to that I'm leaving, I use the computer to type up and print out several signs, in the largest font it could make, "FILL THIS SPACE, I'M GONE, signed..." and then my name and the date. I taped the four copies I made of this on the computer screen, on the desk, on the wall and on the back of my chair.

The only individual left I had to give a 'so long' to was Preston (I don't need to see Mr. Daubens again), who didn't have much to tell me.

"If you get Kyle in your class, you have my permission to push him around," he said, smiling.

"What grade is he in?"

"Fifth. He goes to West Hills, which everyone says is a rough school. He's a bright kid, he'll, I'm sure you'll handle him."

"If I see him, I'll tell him I worked with you."

And that would be the last time I would ever speak to Preston directly again.

———

I went through my checkbook to find out how much was in my account, and with $16,000 or so I feel I have enough to make it for a while. I haven't kept much of an eye on the account or updated the book regularly, which is bad, obviously, but I'm sure that's around where it should be.

———

September 2nd is a lukewarm day so I wear tan Dockers with a cream-colored polo shirt to maximize comfort and match the two colors. I don't intend on wearing a suit or anything of the sort. If the powers-that-be tell me I need certain attire for this job, I suppose I will have to reluctantly follow orders.

Classroom #236, when I arrive at 8:07 AM, has three other people inside besides me (good - this follows my Personal Rule Regarding Lateness), all of them women, all of them at least over forty. The brunette woman seated near the window is wearing a flashy green jacket and blouse, the woman in the far front a redhead with thin straight hair with a purple top and a skirt, the chubby blonde/brunette (it depends on the angle you look at her from) in the second row with all of her baggage strewn about the seats surrounding her, as if creating a magical barrier of personal space.

I seat myself in the far back of the room - away from them - after having them all look at me, each other, then back at whatever else they were originally doing - examining the knife-like scratches in the desks and the cryptic initials engraved there (on my desk there is 'J.S.' <heart> 'S.J.'), checking for runs in stockings, sipping steaming-hot cups of flavored coffee, wincing when it burns taste buds, or looking generally dazed and somewhat distracted. Somewhat.

It wouldn't be until 8:17 when our Introducer (is that a word?) to "The Fine Craft of Teaching" would make her way into the dim, quasi-vacant room, which, eerily enough, is relatively free of children's fingerprints - no pictures/collages on the bulletin boards, no colorful cutouts along the top of the walls, no nauseatingly-simplistic kindergartenese sketched on the blackboard for little eyes to see (I don't think this room has ever housed children, frankly, I think it's just for us "New Recruits"). There is only a blackboard, stained carpet (from footprints and elusive liquids) and twenty-five seats, in five rows of five, filled with three women and me, all waiting for things to get underway.

The woman, a thin, lanky, tall figure (around 6'1") introduces herself as Nicolette - and tells how she's not worked here very long - but enjoys her job as Assistant Chief Instructor for New Personnel. She informs us that the individuals that normally 'run' this class are both away at some conference that's normally in Late September, but there was some problem and they had to set it up earlier and all that's really important is that this 'seminar' will only last one day, instead of three but will go today until 5 or a little later, and the pensive brunette says something about how that's not really "good for her." The two, the Instructor and her, have a brief conversation - Ms. Nicolette tells her to make phone calls at lunch to change whatever very important and vital plan the brunette had planned, but the brunette is not at all pleased with having to "rearrange her whole day" and Ms. Nicolette says she's really sorry and she's just following orders but the brunette just mumbles something and then pulls the old silent treatment by looking out the window. It has been three minutes into the Seminar and already a minor quarrel has risen and swelled.

Ms. Nicolette, brushing this off, resumes with her introduction, explaining exactly how the process works: during the week a woman in Human Resources referred to as the "Substitute Caller" (how *apropos*) will, weeks ahead of time, phone "us," the "Subs," sometimes once a week - sometimes more often - and inform us of the available slots we can fill in for and at what school. We can accept or decline, although frequent declining will probably get you taken off Santa's "Good" List and scribbled on his "Lazy" one.

She then goes through morning procedures - how to "check in" and follow the specific teacher's "Lesson Plans" and how to pen in the slots as to what we accomplished in the day or what still needs to be done, how the children/adolescents behaved, etc. She hands out pieces of paper with everything she says listed on it, all of them being in quite thorough and exacting detail ("Point #6: Proceed to assigned classroom." I'm not kidding). As to why Ms. Nicolette didn't hand these few papers out *before* she explained the protocol so we have something to look at and follow while she spoke is beyond my grasp. I learned in college that during class presentations always make Xeroxes and hand them out *before* the project so the class pays attention to the paper instead of watching you fidget like a Parkinson's patient, sweat profusely over your

DKNY shirt and hear you fight an unwinnable battle with your own quivering voice, which sounds like its jerry-rigged to a dilapidated vibrator. See, I did learn something in college. Thanks, Dad.

More photocopies follow, as I thought there might be, containing, verbatim, most of what she has to say. It's as if someone took every single page of *The Recognitions* and began distributing the whole thing, piece-by-piece, section-by-section, without staples or page numbers. Even while I'm stacking my personal pile, I notice the red-headed woman in the very front row, besides sifting through the handouts, also manage to take notes in a leather-bound notebook that looks expensive. Apparently the side comments Ms. Nicolette makes involving what happens if a child gets sick need to be noted - that pesky "common sense" never does kick in when you need it. Ah, but I am being too critical.

One of the papers I spend my time on is:

How To Deal With Disciplinary Problems

1. Do not yell or use foul language. Stay as calm as possible.
2. Arguing with the child/ren can only make things worse. Resolve conflict or potential conflict with confidence and patience.
3. Do not threaten the child/ren unless you are prepared to follow through.
4. Never, under any circumstances, hit or touch any child/ren.
5. If a fight breaks out, call or contact the Principal or a Police Officer.
6. If a potentially dangerous situation arises, call or contact the Principal or a Police Officer and get children to safety.

What does that "Police Officer" thing mean? Though my memory is hazy, and I did go to Catholic Grade School, I never recall Police Officers being in my school. When punished, at least at my school, you had to stand out in the hall with your back to the classroom. When the teacher had free time, or a break, he/she would go into the hall and deal with the student. I think I was out there - in the hall - a few times, but not many (this may be hard to believe, but true, alas - do not ask me to recall on what grounds I was tossed out there, this, again, I have buried in my head).

My attention refocuses itself and I find my mind back in the room with the others. Ms. Nicolette is describing how class times are constructed, how the day is divided into different subjects (all listed on another handout: "A Typical Day") and time slots (approx. 50 minutes per subject) and about how "we" get breaks whenever they have classes like music, art, library and so on.

At noon we are dismissed to go to lunch, so I get in the car and go to the local shopping center where I have the privilege and freedom to construct my own garden salad with Low Fat Ranch Dressing and sit on the curb outside to eat it, making sure I place three napkins, opened up, right on top of each other on my lap beforehand as to not get anything unsavory on my pants.

The break speeds by entirely too quickly, and I am vaulted back into 236, going over "What To Do In A High School Classroom (And What Not To Do)" (handout #31, I've started counting), which lists more guidelines and rules, for example: "Do not drink alcohol or smoke any substance [!] during class time or in the bathrooms," "Do not go through student lockers," "Do permit students to leave class if they have a Pass," "Do not issue demerits. Allow other teachers to do so," "So get assistance from other faculty and staff if needed," and so forth.

I notice that the brunette that had a fit earlier has not come back from lunch. The other two have, and the redhead in the very front has brought the other half of her chicken salad sandwich in with her, and eats it while examining a hardbound book called, "*Teaching Is Right For You!*", with the "you" part in some cursive font and double underlined as shown. The book has materialized out of nowhere, but I'm assuming it belongs to Ms. Nicolette, who, by the way, may have had a model's lunch of cigarettes and black coffee, and continues to guzzle the coffee from a mug in her skeletal left hand that has a "Virginia is for Lovers" logo printed on it. I look at my own hands after I take note of hers and notice that mine, too, are gaunt, with large knuckles puncturing the thin skin and straw-like bones running lengthwise down each digit. I blame my metabolism.

Ms. Nicolette, later, turns from by-the-book stern pragmatist to confidence-building self-help guru, and gives us a paper on "Being Strict But Fair" (handout #34), which includes statements separated by "bullet points," including: "If you act sheepish the students will not pity you and make the day difficult," "Be confident in who you are and in what you say," "Never yell but be forceful and mature: you are, after all, an adult," and the like.

At the end of the day, 4:45, Ms. Nicolette would take her empty manila folders and empty coffee mug and set us free, with a "Good luck" and "Cheerio." She glazed over the finer points of dealing with the tricky subjects of mathematics and science, about "Teacher's Helpers" who are the "brighter" kids in the class who you can ask for help if you don't know what happens next, established classroom procedure, the paper the Teacher fills out to let you know who has what medical condition and things of that sort. On the back of one of the handouts (#17, "Being Creative"), I drew a quirky picture of Ms. Nicolette surrounded by wide-faced, big teethed, goofy-looking teddy bears defecating but tossed it out.

15.

Ms. Nicolette didn't exactly tell us it wouldn't be until the beginning of October that we'd get phoned for a potential job - the opening weeks of September are usually never open because Teachers need to get their agendas rolling and establishing objectives with their pupils. So for an exaggerated period of time I was left to my own devices, in my apartment, pacing around, chasing away sad ideas, drinking tap water and trying my hand at writing poetry. Mr. Sandburg, Mr. Tennyson: how did you do it? (Favorite line from Tennyson: "I am a part of all that I have met.")

During this time off I also reviewed the papers from the Seminar and tried to make some sense out of this new endeavor of mine. I'm only missing pages #15-17, but I figure they're not totally vital for my purposes.

The phone has been, for the most part, quiet. Sterling did call the one day for about five minutes about baseball or the playoffs or something I don't quite recall to clearly (or fully participated in) because I kept thinking, during the whole 'conversation,' of the report I got and what it said and wanted to say something about it and tried with all of my might to keep my mind away from that. But apart from him, Davis hasn't called, Marie hasn't called, no parents, no anybody. Not even Solicitors feel like trying their hands at me, to convince me to pledge money to some high school or Fund for Some Disease You May Get and We Can't Save You From. Mom, I know, always gets suckered into the way they send her those lick-and-stick address labels and, out of guilt (or perhaps conditioning - someone gives you something, you give something back) donates around $50-100 or so. Pricey labels; crafty Marketing.

Joan the Sub Caller (she is mighty chipper and sounds about 30, but could be one of those Phone Sex Operators who were gifted with the sultry voice of a siren but cursed with the physical form of a stereotypical Housewife) phones me two weeks before I am to start and lines me up for my first week: on Monday I have the 3rd Grade at Chesapeake Grade School, Tuesday and Wednesday at Governor King and Friday Junior English at Justice High School, which I request a change for but she says nothing else is free, everything else was already taken, and tells me I *don't have* to take it, but I suck it up and take it anyway (you know I'm secretly curious).

———

The alarm clock beeps a startling note over and over and over again, sounding more like Mom's office alarm than a wake-up call. I always wanted to splurge and get one of those alarms that plays a song off a CD - I'm sure something by John Lee Hooker might be a fantastic way to start the morning - but simply neglected to journey to the mall. Alas, my chronic laziness has gotten the best of me, my memory the worst and therefore I'm left with what I have.

7 AM had been the time I'd been getting up for my last job, but for the time off I had changed it to 10 AM, which better suits my need for rest. Going *back* to that time is a difficult struggle for me, and my body puts up a great fight - it turns to granite and refuses to budge.

I do all of the necessary morning procedures (after willing myself out of bed and into the bathroom), get in my car, and try to remember where Chesapeake Grade School is located. One of the handouts Ms. Nicolette gave us (a crude but effective map, #6, "Finding Your Way") is somewhere on my kitchen table, but I am too lazy to go back up to my apartment and get it. I make myself a note in the car: bring a backpack/satchel to carry necessary items/books/papers. How could I have humanly forgotten this?

The stupidity continues on and, after driving around for about ten minutes, actually have to ask an old woman in a white (with a single blue stripe) jogging outfit walking a big, gray, shaggy dog that's panting as much as its owner to tell me what direction to head in. She directs me to the proper location (after some mental legwork - she said she has trouble remember street names and I tell her I sympathize) and I arrive at 8:12 - dangerously close to the 8:15 deadline. I find the main entrance, a burgundy steel door (with a "Howdy!" cowboyesque drawing taped to it, made with watercolors and pencil I believe) and step inside. The smell contained within is one of overwhelming dampness, like the lingering scent of moisture after a rainstorm mixed with mildew and mustiness. The walls inside are made of brick, and there are framed pictures of past classes, past principles and school sports teams hung proudly on the main hallway just as you enter. I follow the signs to the Principal's Office where I need to check-in. I'm nervous by the sheer *lack* of commotion - I had envisioned myself being trampled by sprinting second-graders, going to class, waving their backpacks like maces, but none are around.

Inside the Principal's Office I notice a counter running perpendicular to the southernmost wall (where the doorway I enter from is located) with calendars and schedules taped to the front and, on top, a variety of items: a black binder with "Substitute List" written on it, a stack of papers regarding some PTA meetings, a stack of papers regarding some charity or charity-related event and a silver bell sitting idle, waiting to be 'DING'ed.

I glance around the room to see what is a-brew, but alarmingly, there is no one, anywhere. There are simply desks with "Far Side" calendars on them, computer terminals, filing cabinets, manila folders stacked in neat, little piles, a rectangular table with a paper cutter on it (that looks like a castration machine, if I may be so Freudian again), and a clock on the wall that is ten minutes faster than the one on my wrist. East of the main entranceway lies two shut doors, identical in size and shape, but with only one significant difference between them: the door on the left has "Principal " on it, the right "Vice-Principal." Unaware as to whether or not I need to speak to someone before I try to find the classroom, I look for my name in the Substitutes book (it's there, along with 'Room Assigned: 302' and two blank spaces for my name and check-in time), fill that out, and leave the rather spacious office, without succumbing to temptation and hitting the bell.

As I leave I encounter a plain-looking woman in a mauve-colored dress (she's in her early 50s, I'm guessing). I inquire as to where all the children are.

"Are you new?" she asks.

"Yes, actually, I am. I'm a sub for room 302 today and trying to get my bearings."

"Oh, that's Teri's room. The kids-" she looks at her watch, "-won't be here for a while. They get in around 8:45."

"Thank you."

"Good luck!" she tells me.

Room 302, and all its neighboring classrooms, right beside each other, down a long hallway (and up the steps from the Principal's Office, which is on the first floor) are all labeled with little gold plates screwed into their respective doors. The ones running down the left side (my left, at least) are the odds: 101, 201, 301, 401, and down the right, even. The hall is spacious, too, and the roof must be about sixty-feet above me, where some powerful light source emits buzzing rays of light all the way down to me, highlighting every crevice and chip mark in the hall's brick walls. Bulletin boards are hanging next to each classroom, and all are filled with either drawings (the lower grades - 102's features what looks like pictures of children picking strawberries in a field, all done with crayons and marker) or stories (302, my room for the day, has little narratives posted regarding favorite summer activities).

I open the door to 302 and am pleasantly greeted by many Halloween decorations of cardboard cutouts of ghouls/monsters on the walls and black and orange streamers crisscrossing above the blackboard. There are cutout pumpkins on an in-class bulletin board with each pumpkin designed by the students themselves - there are some twenty-five pumpkins in all - and each possesses a different face. One construction paper pumpkin that really catches me is by a girl named Meghan - it has its jagged mouth situated above its eyes (which have spirals spinning freely inside them) and a misplaced square-ish nose carved out of the side of its face. This deformed creature is the most notably abnormal of all the pumpkins, and its creator could very well be a junior Ms. Picasso. I will not mention my admiration for the "piece" to her.

A few other intriguing/typical things in the room, some worth noting, some all together ... *blah*: a chart of Math Strategies, followed by another chart on how to create a line graph, a fuzzy gray wall smothered by newspaper clippings with two columns: one for "National" News and one for "International News" (National is loaded to the point where you cannot tell where one piece ends and another begins - the International column is utterly blank), stacks upon stacks of unorganized papers, folders, grade reports, psychological evaluations, magazines, books in every possible direction and resting in any available free space, and also mini posters with abstract words printed on them and then a quote beneath by some famous individual who is dead and has been dead for a very long time. My favorite:

Persistence:
"Never, never, never, never give up."
-Winston Churchill

The Instructor - Teri somebody - has left her lesson book on top of her desk, which faces about twenty-five seats, placed in an inverted "U" position. I find today's date in the book and run down the assigned list and morning procedures, what she has set up for me and any notes. The first subject is Grammar, followed by Reading (they call it "L.A."), then Science, Spelling, Lunch/Recess, Library, Math and Social Studies. I flip through the texts stacked in the upper-right hand corner of the desk, where she put Post-It Notes in the proper pages, and some comments I skim over because none of them seem relevant or directed at me (they appear to be in there for her, by her).

I sit anxiously yet patiently and wait for the children to arrive, which they do, at 8:50, most of them coming in at once (with a few late stragglers, bless their hearts), find their seats and, all the while, being typical children, "commenting" (loud whispering) to each other about the odd person who is sitting at the front of the class, watching them get organized in silence. Years later, these children will acquire the gift of subtlety, and their "commenting" will be less easy to hear and pick up.

"Good morning," I say, expecting a response. They simply keep looking at me.

"I'm, well, you can call me Devon. I'm the substitute. Ms. ... your teacher is out, so I am filling in. I -," two hands are raised. I call on the girl in the first row, closest to me.

"Yes?"

"Where's Ms. Akagi?"

"I don't know."

"Is she okay?"

"I suppose so. No one told me otherwise."

"She was here yesterday."

"She may be back tomorrow, I don't know. I was only given this class one day, so I'm pretty sure she will be back quickly."

"Oh," she says, before she turns to the girl sitting next to her whom she whispers something to that I can't hear.

"Now somebody please tell me how you start your day off. What are the morning procedures, um - what do you do every morning?"

Someone yells out that we take roll and I ask for a volunteer to do it. One student, Alissa, girl with blonde, braided hair, and a pink pull-over shirt with a giant gold star on it informs me that she always takes roll, so I graciously allow her to do her job (she is Ms. Akagi's Assistant - all Instructors have one, or so I read). Nobody is absent today, nor tardy, so she tells me that she sends it to the main office, so I let her go. After that another student collects lunch money. The children, while this is going on, gradually get louder in terms of vocal pitch, so I ask them to be quiet with the classic "shush" gesture with a finger to the mouth, but they ignore me. I then knock with my fist against the wooden desk, but to no avail. They continue mumbling, which aggravates me to no end, but I promise not to yell or lose control (making reference to Ms. Nicolette's one handout). I simply go over to the blackboard, and begin spending time jotting down the Grammar work assigned for the day, which is working with prefixes. I write several words that have similar prefixes on the board:

untie	recite	indeed
undo	recall	inside
unfair	rewind	indoors

-and proceed to ask someone to start off reading the directions in the text, which actually silences them for a minute while they dig around their belongings for the right book. I reiterate the proper page number several times for those that don't hear me or look lost (I end up just writing it on the board). I call on the one boy who has his book wide open and is looking at me, but he doesn't seem to hear me, exactly. I keep saying, "Yes, you," but nothing.

As I examine all of their faces, I get a general look of dreaminess, which I interpret as a sign of basic fatigue due to having to get up early on a Monday and having to learn things you'd rather you just *knew* and were born with because the process of learning wastes excessive amounts of time (1/3, or twenty two years for most).

Since those I ask to volunteer won't (they just look up at me, then back down to their books), and because there isn't much I can do, and simply looking without saying much at them gets nothing accomplished, I merely opt to read it myself and go over the prefixes on the board myself, going around the inverted "U" one by one until somebody gives me *something*. Their silence, admittedly, makes me even more nervous. It isn't until I accidentally drop the text I was trying to balance in my left-hand that I hear some snickers and I know they're awake.

A long fifty minutes elapse and we move onto Reading. My little Assistant tells me that the class typically breaks into prearranged small groups to work on stories in the text, do summary questions and engage in discussion. There are three groups: the Lions, the Tigers and the Bobcats. It doesn't take long to figure out that the Lions are the "accomplished" readers, with the Tigers being the middle-of-the-roaders and the Bobcats those left behind. The Teacher's notes suggest I make my rounds to each group, observing and taking notes and ensuring that work is being done (no goofing around), but to avoid favoritism I neglect to fulfill these obligations. When I give the assignments to each group, I get a lot of puzzled faces and mumbling going on - the assignments aren't understood by anybody, and each group looks at me like I came from another classroom with completely different texts and page numbers - and one even goes as far as asking, "What are you talking about?" I repeat the assignment, show them the text and point to the exact page, after which they say things like "We're supposed to skip that," or "We did that" and I just say "just do it or do it again" and retreat towards the desk and sit and let them be, ignoring raised hands and instructing them to "figure it out together."

I do make obligatory rounds every ten minutes or so, acting like I'm following their every move like a hawk, but for all intensive purposes they don't care. In fact, when the Reading time slot comes to an end, the middle group (the Tigers) ask me if I want to examine their notebooks - the whole lot of them rising and crowding my desk. I quickly shoo them away, as they feel like a murder of crows swooping around all angles, with papers pushed in front of my face, handing me black books with simplistic and half-hearted print in them. (As a note: this would not be the only time students gather around me, asking me something, complaining of some insidious virus that attacks young stomachs right after lunch/recess, asking questions that range from the inane to the inane, etc. I don't know if they're sucking up to me or just like to be out of their seats. Considering I don't believe the former - what I say or think means little - I tend to point to the latter).

Science comes and stays for what feels like an eternity and a day and then some and then longer and this, once again, involves me reading from the book, asking more questions, trying to make things clear - and maybe they do get them, but they never exactly show it. The only real question/statement I get from anyone is courtesy of a boy in a Adidas T-shirt, sporting a Dutch-boy haircut regarding the sun and how it acquired its 'name,' and I admitted I had no clue and spent a good deal of time looking through the index trying to find the elusive answer ... but none could be found. I think it has something to do with mythology, I tell him, and he nods.

... And Spelling is the subject after Science. Nothing to add there, except one incident in which two of the boys in the back of the room keep kicking the legs of another boy's chair they are seated to the right and left of, respectively, but the boy keeps writing in his notebook, visibly unfazed. It takes me to step in and give the glare-of-death at the other two, and I threaten to move their seats. They desist temporarily. Also, while I sit down and let them work privately on their printing in their workbooks, a bunch of them come to the front and ask to use the bathroom. I let each of them go, one at a time, until the entire class has to go, and I scoot them back into their chairs and tell them to hold it until lunch.

Lunch break is free time for me to go to the Teacher's Lounge (that we were all enthralled by when I was a student - what's in there? a TV? a stereo? exercise equipment?). But before I head over there I have to lead the kids down to the cafeteria, single file (an ideal which they naturally stray from). I don't know what is being served today, but the scent is strong and I'm guessing it's something like tacos or sausage sandwiches and it's making me nauseous. Since I didn't bring lunch with me, I leave to go to the grocery store's food court to buy (and make!) my salad and grab a bottle of spring water and also get some grocery shopping done. I realize I wasn't supposed to leave, but ah, I figure, let them tell me.

After lunch the kids have recess and library, which the Instructor wrote that I don't have to worry about since the Librarian or the Assistant to the Librarian usually corrals the wandering kids, who are playing in the courtyard out back.

I make myself a much-needed cup of coffee while in the Teacher's Lounge - it's not Instant, but the machine isn't exactly made by Bunn. I continue to be mad at myself for not bringing a book to read or something to draw on, perhaps under the dense notion that I would be allotted no break time.

Surprisingly enough I haven't seen many other teachers out and about today, which I dismiss as alternative scheduling on their part (sort-of like the wife who works days and the husband who works nights, and the two don't see each other but to pass in their garage, give a kiss that signifies both hello and goodbye, and make on their merry way, unfazed by the disjointed nature of their relationship).

I rest in the chair in the "Lounge," which, by the way, is a big disappointment - neither TV, nor stereo, nor exercise equipment like Soloflex or NordicTrack, no perks, no library of sophisticated fiction and non-fiction, no humidor, no sofa, no massage chair. It's basically a poor, poor man's apartment: several (3) banged-up and torn plush blue chairs (the one I'm seated in has fistfuls of padding yanked out in the back by my left shoulder), all of which gather around a circular, coffee-mug stained rickety wood table, an empty filing cabinet in the corner (I wonder as to what it may have originally held), a metal stool in the middle of the room that's really out-of-place, and a coffee table placed near no coffee nor no chair with the latest magazines on top - mostly *Time*, *Newsweek*, *Sports Illustrated*, *National Geographic* and a really, really out-of-place *Rolling Stone*.

The refrigerator, which is by the sink and coffee pot, is rancorous and quite unsanitary inside (I opened it up out of curiosity) - inside there are near-frozen (or completely-frozen) food bits and liquid compositions spilled all over the place, along the walls and on the top of the shelves, there's a bowl of fuzzy, moldy assorted fruit, a black cup with an unidentifiable substance within, a brown paper bag containing who-knows-what ... I cease my investigation and go back to the chair, my legs antsy and nervous, worried I may have done something wrong earlier or said something wrong, anxious because I don't know what on Earth I'm doing here, yet strangely disconnected from my doubts simultaneously: I *try* to weigh all emotions equally. Consider all!

16.

As it turns out, the rest of that day went, for the most part, fairly smoothly (one young man decided to whittle his wooden ruler into a knife, which I had to confiscate, another boy wanted to do cartwheels in the empty hallways, forcing me to go out and drag him back inside the classroom). The collective mood of the children, in general, was wildly bizarre - most were either dead silent or spent all day mumbling quietly to themselves (I could not make out what they were saying). When they were supposed to be reading from, say, the Science text, they colored and used markers on their desks, arms and clothes. I marked cleanly in the Teacher's Lesson Plan what I covered subject-wise. I made no mention of the children.

The real problem hits on Wednesday, the second day I'm at Governor King, 5th Grade. Like all "problems" it lands right in my lap, blindsiding me, while I'm teaching the New England colonies in Social Studies to the class as a whole (which, again, involves me sitting and reading aloud, stopping if anyone is talking, walking around). Anyway, I'm simply looking down, discussing 'Revolution' this and 'Tea Party' that, and going on and on, and at the end of the section I look up and get ready to pry a little bit of something out of them when my eyes immediately shift to a boy in the back of the room with a gray Polo shirt on and Dockers lying on the floor, twitching frantically, head jerking back and forth, forward and backward, as if being pulled by a string in every direction, his body curled in a semi-fetal position. I don't know how long he's been doing that - I was reading for quite some time - and none of the children in the class bother to say anything. They merely keep their eyes facing forward or fixed on their texts. I rush over to him to try to get help, murmuring "Oh fuck," and "What happened," and "Who did this," and "What's going on," out loud, over and over again. I go over to him and his eyes are closed, but I don't touch him because I don't know what to do. I keep asking him if he's all right, but he doesn't respond. I scramble over to the class phone to call the Nurse. I ask the boy nearest to the ill child to watch him. I pick up the phone, but don't know any of the proper numbers (I try 9-1-1, but the phone won't allow for outside numbers). I ask the class what the Nurse's number is, but those that look up just shrug or say, "I don't know." I open the classroom door to start yelling "Help" to *anyone*, but all the doors in the hall I'm in are shut, and since they're wooden and have no glass panes in them I can't see inside. I try opening all of them but they're either locked or, if open (only one is), there's no one inside.

When I return to the room I see the boy is sitting up and rubbing his eyes and (I think) crying softly. I go over to him and I ask if he's okay and all he tells me is a garbled, "I'm sorry" and I tell him it's no trouble at all but we have to go to the nurse or hospital if need be. He shrugs - what can he say? I tell the class' young Teacher's Helper (another charming blonde female, this one's Tania) to ensure there is no raucousness in the room while I am gone, and forewarn the class to be on their best behavior.

As we walk down the hallways, which are wide but poorly-lit, I make conversation with the boy, who tells me his name is Gardner (I tried jogging briskly whilst holding his hand, but he kept pulling away from me, determined to take his own sweet time).

"What was that all about?"

He looks up at me. "That happens sometimes."

"How often?"

"It depends."

"Have you been to a doctor?"

"Yeah, he gave me pills, but they don't work."

"Where are those pills? You need them, right?"

"I guess," is all he says.

I tell him about how he seemed fine yesterday when I taught the same class.

He takes a handkerchief out of his pocket, blows his nose, looks at it, folds it back up and puts it in his pants pocket. "Can I go to the bathroom?"

"Sure, sure. Go ahead," I say, warily, timing him in case he has another episode and I have to go in after him. I hope I'm handling this all right.

While he's inside I pace around the hallway with an eye on my watch and another looking out for other Teachers.

He quickly comes out and we head for the Nurse's Office. I ask him if he messed his clothes and he says no.

The Nurse's Office is by the school's "Music" room, and the door is open so we head right in. The desk to the right is stockpiled with notes and memos, a Mickey Mouse clock, a computer that's up and running, the hum filling the room with noise, as well as other assorted paraphernalia. On a table right behind the desk is the standard medical table with a jar of tongue depressors, a box of powdered rubber gloves, cotton swabs in a pink ceramic bowl and drawers underneath with presumably more equipment like blood-pressure cuffs, stethoscopes, thermometers, gauze, Band-Aids. Behind that table is a large blue curtain that goes from ceiling to floor, covering the width of the room. Despite all this, I still see no Nurse.

"Where is she?" I ask Gardner. He tells me she's usually in on Wednesdays.

I wander around the back, behind the blue curtain, but only find a small cot with a white blanket and pillow on it. On the adjacent wall is a laminated poster of young puppies with baskets in their mouths filled with daisies and flowers of assorted colors. It reads, "Get Well Real Soon."

I back out the sleeping area and see Will wandering the hallways, looking for potential assistance. He suggests we try the Principal's Office, so we do.

Inside the Office, there is an elderly woman with pink-framed bifocals and a heavily sprayed dome-like hairstyle. We ask her where the nurse is.

"Isn't she in there now?"

"No. We just checked. This young man needs the nurse or his parents right away."

"Is he sick?" she asks.

"Yes. Can you call around to find somebody?"

She nods. "You're not the regular Teacher are you?"

"Nope. And never had to deal with something like this."

Gardner is definitely calmer than I, reading the bulletin board next to the office desk and pacing around, kicking a floor-bound paper clip. The lady starts making phone calls.

I turn to the boy. "What do they normally do when this happens?"

Without taking his eyes off the paper clip, he answers, "The Nurse calls my Mom and sends me back to class. I go to the doctor later."

"They don't send you to the hospital?"

"I was there a long time ago, the first time."

"How long have you had this? All your life?"

"Just the last couple of years."

I turn back to the lady. "What's going on?"

She shakes her head. "I can't find anyone. I called the Nurse's office, the cafeteria, the Teacher's Lounge - do you think I should call his parents?"

"Why are you asking me? I don't know." I redirect the question to Gardner. He tells us he'll just inform his parents when he gets home.

"Do we need an ambulance? Call 9-1-1." I tell her.

"Shouldn't we wait to see what the Nurse says?" the lady asks.

"What Nurse?"

Gardner speaks up. "I'm fine. Really."

I sigh. "What if that happens again?"

"Why don't you just leave him here for the time being," the lady says, "and I'll eventually get someone on the phone and we'll take it from there. If nothing turns up I'll call the hospital. What's his full name and grade?"

I call Gardner over and he gives the information, as well as his phone number. The lady goes over to the computer.

"Do you have someone covering your class?" she asks me.

"No. Couldn't find anyone free or otherwise."

"Then I'll take care of this."

"Are you sure?" I'm a little tentative to leave.

"Go." She waves me away.

I tell Gardner I'm going and to get better soon and I shake his hand but he assures me he's coming back to class later.

While I had feared pandemonium would have struck at this point, complete with antics out of a Golding novel (pig heads on stakes, war paint), I was relieved to know they had managed to keep it to a dull roar, with Tania the Little Teacher's Helper, sitting at the Instructor's class with a laser pointer she found someplace, acting as Mother Hen to try to keep things in line, which I thank her for. Some of the kids managed to go into the Teacher's desk, grab colored chalk and completely decorate the boards with pictures, faces and messages (one reads: "Everything you do smiles back at you"), some have gathered in packs around the PCs in the back of the class, some are playing cards with actual cards for what I think is real money in the one corner (which I find to be educational, others hold a lesser opinion of). They don't seem to notice I've found my way back into the room.

Eventually Tania and I corral them back into their seats. They beg me not to erase the blackboards and to leave their drawings alone. I promise, but now have no place to write assignments or examples.

As for Gardner, he would, like he said, come back to the room after Lunch/Recess. I asked him how things went and if they found the Nurse but he doesn't say and just asks me what he missed in class.

Neither Nurse nor the lady in the Principal's Office ever phoned the room to tell me what happened. It would have been nice to know that Gardner had this problem - according to Ms. Nicolette's handouts, the Class Instructor is to notify all Substitutes of what students have what medical problems and what medicine they take.

17.

I opt to keep the high school assignment on Friday (after having all of Thursday - my day off - to mull it over), but show up fifteen minutes later than I should have, forcing the main office to call the School District to determine where I am. I inform the woman managing the Main Office's counter and telephones that she shouldn't call anyone and that I will always arrive prompt and ready and she says she simply can't do that because what if I'm not there and they have to cover themselves. I told her that it was a train this morning that impeded my forward progress but she obviously doesn't believe me even though it's sort-of the truth.

In all honesty, it's a major shock (a better term: déjà vu) to return to high school. For someone in their mid-twenties, the sight of seeing teenagers strolling around hallways, laughing, misbehaving ('we ought not all misbehave, but we ought to look as if we could' - thank you, Mr. Welles), planning futures or ignoring it all together. Frankly, I'd rather stick to grade school in terms of instruction, as with young kids you could foul something up and they honestly couldn't tell the difference.

Today, I remembered to carry along a tan satchel I bought at some 5 & 10, and put in the following items: eye drops, a folder filled with plain white paper to sketch on, two pencils (in desperate need of sharpening and only one with an eraser) and lunch (a pear, an apple, a banana,

Dannon Vanilla Yogurt, a warm bottle of Aquafina). I should have brought a book to read, but did not.

The hallways smell a lot like the food already being cooked up in the cafeteria below (my guess: something with onions) covered up or masked with random splish-splashes of cologne and wondrous scented sprays which gathers together, in one monstrous cloud, inside the classrooms, and seeps out the vents at the bottom of the door and wanders about the hallways freely, unhindered. Above my head, a few feet, there are steel pipes running in M.C. Escheresque patterns, criss-crossing at will, burrowing into and out of holes in the ceiling. They produce a "gurgling" noise as gushes of liquid make their way from all directions, running along the pipes, weaving back and forth, down the length of the hall, until meeting the end of their journey and temporarily finding solace, someplace, only to be replaced by more gushes sometime later.

The sound of teenage noise stifles the surges, talking, slamming lockers, gum snapping, shoes tapping the plain white floor, which is covered in hair and dust and streaked by black scuffmarks. In the hall I'm in (to the right of the main office - it's Junior Hall), people are walking to wherever, never alone but always in a pack, looking around. While I've never been in this school before, the room I'm assigned to is easy to find (#368), and, like everyplace else, has the numbers on the door in gold lettering.

Inside, my nerves take hold of me as thirty-odd kids sit in their assigned seats, fidgeting, chatting. I tiptoe in as to not make some grand entrance. As I go over to the desk (without saying "Hello" or "Good Morning"), I pass by a young lady who must have taken a bath in some Vitamin-E Enriched strawberry-scented body lotion, as the smell is dense and heavy and almost makes you want to choke (it has caused some of the male deer around her to pay extra attention, so I presume it's served its purpose).

As it turns out, the Instructor I'm replacing not only has Junior English 1 and Senior English 2, but also homeroom to take care of as well, checking for attendance and tardiness. Junior English runs first and third periods, Senior English fifth, sixth and eighth (there are only eight periods). As for right now, homeroom is my only priority.

I hear laughing as soon as I sit down in the Teacher's chair, with my head down, paranoia telling me the laughter is directed *at* me, while rationality meanwhile says that such thoughts are egotistical and reflect a potentially held belief that I am the focus of others' constant attention. It isn't local laughing, isolated to one subsection of the room, like, say, the front right corner. It's sounds fairly widespread - that is, until I raise my head from the paper I was pretending to start counting heads (had I looked up earlier they would have known it bothered me). When I do look out to the sea of desks, all I see are heads, some smiling, some not, some playing with pens or pencils, some not, some plagued by skin problems, some with amazing skin, some dolled up with mascara and eyeliner and every other type of smoke and mirror Clinique sells, some trying to sculpt their *already* receding hairlines (so young, too!) to look like movie stars or athletes or models or 7 ½ minute famers, some chewing gum, some chewing on pens, some thinking they're someone they're not, some not thinking at all.

"Are all of you in alphabetical order? Whose seat is that?" I ask, pointing to the one vacant seat situated in the dead center of the room.

A well-built, lanky fellow with curly blonde hair tells me that they are not in alphabetical, just seated randomly. There are thirty-six seats, six rows of six, all facing forward, with thirty-five of them filled. The name of the girl that's out is Alice something.

"Doesn't she have hepatitis?" one girl suddenly asks another, seated directly behind her, an aside but loud enough for everyone to hear. "I heard that a few days ago."

"No," another answered, down a row and to her left, "isn't it cancer? Lymph-something? That's what Sam said."

"Jeff said he had no idea," the one who originally started this replies.

"But I thought it was cancer," another in the back says.

"Did anyone go to visit her?" someone else asks.

This conversation, initially started with just a few, gathers steam and attracts the attention of the whole class, one by one, all of which starts bickering as to what pieces of the puzzle each overheard carries any weight (as well as comparing notes and insider information). One young man thinks she's in Philadelphia being treated for a serious intestinal problem, another says she's at Johns Hopkins, others disagree and say she moved out of town, and the whole pseudo-discussion goes on and on and gets louder so I start saying "Nevermind" over and over to settle them down. I ask when homeroom ends since the Instructor's notes are vague. They eventually calm themselves and I get an answer: it ends in ten minutes. Fine.

I mark down on the Absentee paper "1." I put a "0" next to "Tardy," as I'm sure this only relates to the students, ho ho.

The bell rings and they scurry out, backpacks and notebooks in hand. In funnels my first class, Junior English 1.

This group is currently reading *Antigone*, which I myself studied some time ago when I was in high school. The assignment is for the whole class to read Part 1 of the play, aloud, and discuss the usage of the following in the work: "character," "mood," "personification," "theme," "the usage of metaphors and allusions" and the concept of "tragedy" in the theatre. In recollection, now that I have time to really think back, I don't recall doing all that fantastic in English (roughly B, B-), and some of these "components" of storytelling are a little vague to me, so I force myself to review the text and definitions quickly before I have to teach it.

In each Junior English class there are no more than, say, 15-20 kids in the room, nor are there reading groups like in grade school. All of them are to face forward, look at me, answer questions I ask, not discuss anything with each other and only with me and to read the matter, different people taking different parts (that I pick them for - no one volunteers). Most of their readings carry little or no conviction behind them - one young man's rendition (in period 3) of a bubbling cauldron that is Creon is merely carbon fizzling from a Coke can, blurting lines like, "Money! Money's the curse of man, none greater," with no concept of fury involved. I'm not asking for Olivier or Jacobi, but slight interest in the matters at hand might encourage one to enjoy the story more, is all. Or at least, a little inflection may make me yawn less, despite ten-plus hours of rest last night. In the hallways, they think they're actors/actresses. In their homes, they think they're actors/actresses. In dealing with each other, they're actors/actresses. Why not now?

The other class, the one with Seniors, is reading Charlotte Perkins Gilman's short story *The Yellow Wallpaper*, an insidious tale of a woman suffering from terrible anxiety, depression, tension, jitteriness (perhaps she's best labeled as psychotic, or at least hopelessly neurotic) and is fighting a jagged battle with her surroundings. For this tale I had the students take turns reading aloud, one taking one page, another student the next and so forth. At the end we (rather, I) analyzed the John character - the woman's husband - and narrator's character, the imagery, the ending.

During my lunch break I sit in Justice High's Teacher's Lounge in the Senior Hallway, upstairs and above the Junior hallway. Inside, I devour my homemade lunch and simultaneously draw geometric shapes on white pieces of paper, with circles overlapping squares and triangles fondling rhombuses. Not exactly aware of those coming in and out of the room, I become startled when a man sneaks behind me and inquires as to what I am scrawling. I tell him it's "simply random stuff, nothing in particular," and he emits an "Oh," and goes to the refrigerator nearby to take out a Sprite. He comes and sits at the same table I'm seated at, but across from me and not facing my direction. He cracks open the top, and commences guzzling.

In between intakes he sets the can down on the counter, forming a ring of aluminum can sweat on the hardwood table. Then he drags the can around, extending the run and transforming into a tube, spins it around in a circle, plays with the tab, runs his finger through the water on the table, and looks up.

"You a Sub?"

"Yessir. Never been here before."

"Oh."

I go back to drawing and my half-eaten apple.

"Who are you in for?" he inquires, filling the silence.

"Junior and Senior English. Deborah somebody."

"Right, right," he says, nodding, continuing to look around the room, his body turned 45° and his back to the window. The shirt he's wearing, a forest green button down, is meticulously ironed; his light green tie (which matches the shirt) has a metallic clasp holding it to the shirt. His hair is a painstakingly combed ornament, resembling the slicked-and-polished style popular in Mr. Gable's era. Not a single facial hair can be seen.

"Oh - my name's Mr. Metz. I teach Bio." He stretches out his right hand, manicured as expected.

"Devon." I extend mine after looking at his hand for a bit. We shake, his being a firm grip, and warm.

"What do you think?"

"I think it's too early to tell to be honest with you."

"It's not hard," he says, as he finished the Sprite, breaks off the tab, puts it in his shirt pocket and gets up to toss the can in the green Recycling container across the room. "You get used to it. After a short time, you get over the jitters. You know how to handle everything, teach everything, make everyone happy."

"Can I ask you something?"

"Go right ahead."

"Is it just me, or does everyone seem...? You know. They're not real friendly."

"I wouldn't say that. You don't know them. They're just young. It's tough - you remember."

I scratch my hair, which is itchy. "Do you like teaching?"

He tilts his head to the left, slightly shrugs his shoulders. "Some days. It has its incentives. My wife helps me grade papers, make tests, do stuff like that. You have leeway with how you handle your class. It isn't a bad career - at least I think so. Been doing it for 16 years now. Still a kid at it, though. Some have been here longer."

"But I thought all teachers got burned out after tenure."

He laughs. "Some, some. Those that take it too seriously can. One - one woman, she taught algebra," he says as he adjusts the tie clasp and brushes the mystery fuzz off his pants, "she couldn't deal with the tedium and rude kids and the other teachers and went back to school to take up computers or something. Or did she get another job? No, no, she's the one who went for computers. This was years ago, about ten, and I saw her since and she told me she likes what she's doing. If you take it all to heart, you'll hate it."

———

Period 7 with Senior English is intriguing in one respect and startles me in a way I didn't really think about (all blows do seem to be struck left-handed). I'm sitting behind the desk, going down the class list, not paying attention to much else, just calling out names, when, after "Secund," the name, "Stride, Elizabeth," and my heart goes piddy-pat with perverse recognition - the girl from Sterling's report. When I announce her name, I force myself to look up and around to see her (but with caution - one must not come across as being creepy or bizarre) to get a visual image. What is she doing? Is she reading her book? Is she adjusting her clothing? No, she's just sitting, as she should.

Ms. Stride is an excessively petite, square-faced figure, who is wearing tasteful amounts of makeup, rouge and lipstick (at least, from where I'm seated, about fifteen feet away) as well as tactful attire (charcoal gray sweater, deep black jeans). Her eyes are bright and alarming, not to mention attentive - she isn't slouching or brooding, doesn't carry the visible baggage of one who was hurt many times, but then again she may possess that in-born gift of resilience, the ability to walk away and recover.

(Wait: what am I saying? Should she be wearing a hat with the word "Victim" printed on it? What's wrong with me?)

She answers "Here" without any hesitation - as if she were actually paying close attention to class proceedings. Some of the others require their names to be called over and over again until someone near them taps them or they snap to and bring themselves back into the classroom.

I make sure to call on her to do a page in "The Yellow Wallpaper," so I get a good chance to hear her voice, listen to her pronunciation, her inflection - not for any good reason, but merely out of curiosity. She speaks no better nor no worse than her peers in this class or previous periods, no softer not louder, no more hasty, her voice no more feminine nor whispery.

Since I called on her to read, afterwards I do not pick on her to answer any discussion questions to avoid suspicion. But all the while, in the deep recesses of my thinking, my piecing together the fragments, trying to reconstruct the incident, I keep wondering why why why *this person*, why *at all*. And I keep wondering *is it her* and if it is how will I know or why I'm even bothering to care at all - let everything go - but I cannot, the curiosity has me.

After class ends and the hall bell rings and they scoot out the door, off to find peers and their lockers and their next classes, I muster the will to drag Ms. Stride over to me with an "I'm sorry but your name, it sounds so *familiar*" which I realize looks like a frat-ish pickup line and could be interpreted as something more than I intend it to be (I have never developed proper "pick-up" skills, although I think that "gift" comes from a combination of self-obsession and predatory intent).

She turns to me, her purse and Lancôme tote bag slung over her right shoulder. "Hmmm?" is all she replies.

"Your name. It sounds really familiar. I just keep thinking about where I know it from and it's really really bothering me - um, I hope I'm not being a pest," I say as I wave my feet around under the desk.

"Maybe you live near us."

"I don't think so, I live, real far away." I think back to the case and my weak long-term memory. "I think I know your parents, because...."

"There are a lot of Strides around."

"Yeah. Yeah. Forget it. I'm so sorry. You'll be late for your last class."

But I've drawn her in. "Do you bowl?"

"No."

"Because my parents belong to a bowling team at the '7-10 Club.' Maybe from there."

"They don't do stuff like that - never mind," I say, waving my hands around, "I'm just being a pest, here."

She ignores that. "My Dad's an accountant. And my Mom's-"

"An accountant?"

"Yes."

"His name...?"

"Everybody calls him, well, everyone calls him Jim."

"Nope, Jim doesn't sound familiar."

A pause. "It's not his real name. His real name is Nate but he doesn't like it. James is his middle name."

"Hmmm ... you know - that could be it," I say.

"My Mom's a hairstylist."

"I'm pretty sure your Dad is my parents' accountant." I smack the desk. "That's where. That ever happen to you? Like, you hear a name, and you think and think and it, you draw a complete blank. It drives you crazy if you just *dwell* on it. You know?"

"Oh yes," she smiles. It's quite a charming smile too - the dimples add to the effect.

"I'm sorry, again," I laugh, "do you need a late slip? I can..." I shuffle through the desk drawers, "I can find you one."

"No," she waves me off, "History's down a few doors. How long's he been their accountant?"

"For ... how long has he been doing it?"

"Ten, twelve years."

"Well, then, since the beginning, or a year after. He was recommended by a friend."

"He worked for his first three years in Manhattan."

I stopped for a moment. "Then I guess it was after that - I'm really not sure of all the details. I only overheard them mention him it a long time ago - I have my own place now. I think they still go to him." 'My own place?' Oh, man.

"Do you want me to check? Your last name is Devon, right?" She starts going around her purse for a pen.

"No, well, no, you don't have to. It's really, you should go to class."

"I insist. I'll ask. That's 'on' right, not 'en.'" She found paper, too, and is writing it down.

"What?"

"For Devon."

"Don't - it's an 'o,' - and don't worry about it, you go to class, and thanks again," I tell her, as she finishes writing something down. "It was just, just a question, you know."

"How long are you subbing here?" she asks as she paces towards the door.

"Just today. Just today."

"All right."

"Hope you liked the story," I say.

"I did," she says, as her sandals carry her feet out the door and into the musty hallway where she disappears.

The next period I basically make the students conduct their own, having them do all the reading and questions in silence while I rummage through the Instructor's paperwork and grade book for Ms. Stride's grades and how many times she's been absent, late, etc. Doubts still form in my mind - is this the same girl? Is there a chance it isn't? She mentioned her mother - I should have gotten her first name while I was at it.

From what I can find (the Instructor keeps horrendous notes, mostly chicken scratch and personal memos - one curious one has a message to call the doctor about a rash"), Ms. Stride is in good academic standing (though it is only October), with perfect attendance (all check marks under each of the class dates) and two good quiz scores: an 88 and a 94 (one on Sept 17th, the other Sept. 26th).

I also check in the phone book in the Instructor's desk and look up "Stride." It lists four separate first names at five separate addresses. "Nathan" is not among them, but nor is it in the Yellow Pages, under "Accountants."

It is a mystery I tell you! But I am intent on clearing the brush and rampaging through.

18.

"You prying *shit*," Sterling snarls at me in the deepest, most hostile voice he can produce, eyes flaring, nails digging deep into the palms of his fists. We're at "The Limelight," a bar/restaurant located on 4th Street. It's relatively vacant, which I attribute to the fact that it is only Tuesday night. There are cubicle-type booths for people to sit in, with random etchings carved into the aligning walls, most of them uncreative/typical cliches: 'X + Y 4EVR,' or 'Call _____ for a quick fuck,' or '<last name>, <year of carving>' (ex: Heitmann 92) or just random initials for those too frightened or lazy to include the whole name. A small, low-watt white lamp bolted to the sidewall is the only form of illumination available to us.

"The Limelight" is your typical bar: dark, moody, noisy (not from people, but from the jukebox, which is emitting some obnoxious Bob Marley song endlessly, as if on a constant loop). The Bouncer by the door is a short but beefy fellow who wears flannel and a Pittsburgh Pirates hat - he's actually quite the nice guy, and one night about a year ago Sterling and Davis struck up a conversation with the Bouncer over cigars, and the Bouncer even wound up giving Davis a free Dunhill which Davis volunteered to pay for but the Bouncer said was on him. I don't know why he gave Davis the cigar, and I never asked him.

I have made the exceptionally wise decision to not call and bring along Davis - I feel that mainly speaking to

Sterling one-on-one will increase the air of "privacy" and "secrecy," and, inside a loud bar, who cares?

Sterling is drinking a beer, I have ice water.

"What did I tell you? Didn't I kindly fucking ask for you to simply leave this alone?" Sterling, I misjudged, cares a lot.

"Aw, come on, man. You went to a member of *my family* to cover the case. Then you say I can't know anything. That's insulting to me, isn't it? If you wanted to completely keep it all hush-hush, you could have found another lawyer. You can't swing a dead cat around without nailing one of them."

"You *know why* I went to her."

"Yes, yes. Your Mom and her, long history together, yes, yes, I know. I realize that. I've known you for how long?"

"Why do you always feel you need to know everything, huh? You know how you get. I don't need more criticism or ethics thrown at me."

"So ... it happened?"

He doesn't answer.

A waitress in the corner of my eye makes her way to the table, stops a few feet away, holding a black circular serving tray in both hands in front of her, hears the pitch of our voices and the potential war, and shuffles away slowly determined not to interrupt the fray.

I start up again. "To me, it seemed as if everyone was treating it-"

He interrupts. "How did you find out?"

"Let me put it this way: no one told me."

"Was it Davis?"

"No. I broke in and stole your record."

He just looks at me. He scratches the back of his head near his neck. "Broke in?"

"Put on black clothing, at night, went in the office through the back window."

"The office? You're joking."

"Nope."

"Don't you have a key?"

"Nope."

"Isn't there an alarm?"

"Yes."

"Didn't the police come?"

"I assume."

"Did they see you?"

"I hid in bushes blocks away."

"And she never found out."

"I don't think so, because I found my way back in after photocopying everything - the alarm was off again - returned the original and snuck out the back again."

"You're lying."

"Not at all. And get this: on my way home, in all black, driving real slow, these cops stop me, and I'm thinking 'I'm dead' but they just give me this stub for running a stop sign."

"You were so cautious you missed the sign."

"I guess."

He shakes his head, while looking at the bottom of his beer bottle. "I can't ... believe you."

"That's not the real thing: I got the report, read it and the transcript, and all about the girl. Get this: I was teaching at this high school, and in my one class, I saw her."

"Oh Jesus."

"And I talked to her. Thin, dimples, brunette. At least, I think it's her. Her father's name matches, don't know her mother's-"

His anger resurfaces after a slight cool-down period. "Exactly *what* did you say to her? If you mentioned-"

"Whoa, whoa, whoa, hold on. I played it as innocently as I could. I said her name sounded familiar, and-"

"Oh ... why did you have to say anything?"

"Was it her?"

"I don't know and I don't care," he says, dismissively.

"She's a good reader, too," I say, and smile.

"Yeah, yeah, whatever, look, you have to just drop this. Now."

"I understand," I tell him, "I understand her story, which I read, is different from yours. But some of it *has* to be based on fact."

"You weren't even *there*. I'm not sure what you read, but I'm sure it makes me sound like a complete misogynist."

"Are you?"

"Don't do that."

"Choking?"

"No, now..."

"Hair pulling?"

He rubs his eyes with the palms of his hands, and I lean back to avoid getting hit. He doesn't, though. "It's ... exaggerated."

"That's what I thought you'd say."

"The whole thing, I'm just taking the blame because she got home late and her friends said she was with me, and then her parents ... wait - why am I explaining this to you?"

He swivels around in his seat, pokes his head above the high cubicle-type wood seat (with leather padding which has been reupholstered half-a-dozen times, I'm guessing) to scan the room for a waitress. "Where did she go?"

I flick soggy napkin pieces around with my thumb and forefinger. "She was here a bit ago but heard us and backed off."

"How could she hear anything with that '60s shit playing?"

I shrug. "Frankly, I have a hard time hearing *you* clearly."

"Yeah."

There's a brief pause here - he rustles in his seat, I stare at the table.

"Out of curiosity-" I start.

"Don't."

"No, it's not about you."

"That's good."

"Where was Davis the whole time? It doesn't say in the papers. He and-"

"Eric."

"Right, he and Eric were there too."

"And what were they doing?"

"We don't follow each other around. We're all grownups."

"I was just wondering."

"They were downstairs."

"You know something? Marie was asking me what Davis was doing there with you. She wanted to find out, I guess, if he was cheating on her."

"So you were doing this for her?" he asks.

"No, I refused to tell her what I found out."

He shakes his head. "I never did like her."

He continues turning around, looking for someone, anyone, to come by and get us more drinks.

I slump back in my chair and murmur to myself, which, of course, he can hear over the music.

"What?"

"Hmm?"

"You said something."

"It's nothing."

"Let's have it."

"You don't want to hear it."

"I know I don't."

"Really." I'm trying to let him off the hook.

"Say it."

"She is really too damn young."

He looks me right in the eyes and then leans back and slides the beer back and forth between his hands, his face is bright red. "You know the worst part?"

"No."

"Now I'm a Sex Offender. That - that's what bothers me."

"Hasn't AT&T done anything?"

"Like?"

"Fired you?"

"No."

"Said anything?"

"I don't think they can if they knew."

Something by the Dave Matthews Band starts playing on the CD System/Jukebox. Sterling leans over to look at the jukebox down the long aisle. "I like this one."

"What about the millions she's suing you for?"

"Mrs. ... sorry, your Mom says they aren't seeing a nickel of that."

"How does she know?"

"I really don't know. When she talks to me, I swear I can't understand a word she's saying. I just nod."

"She's been doing this a long time," I say before I drink down the rest of the lukewarm tap water. "I *guess* she knows what she's doing."

"I need you to promise me something."

"Sure," I say. "What?"

"I don't want you to ever mention this again, do you hear me?"

"I won't."

"To *anyone.*"

"I swear."

"All right." He nods.

"You know something?" I say. "I think we're all allowed moments of weakness. You know?"

"I don't think so," he tells me.

"Oh," I say, as I look at the ice melting in my glass.

There's an extended pause and I get up to go to the bar and buy another Heineken and get another glass of water.

When I return to our seat I give him his drink and tell him it's on me.

"Now," I start over, "how's Annie doing?"

He smiles.

19.

For the rest of October and November I continue on my teaching ways, slowly becoming more and more adroit at conducting class, overcoming some nervousness (not entirely, but to some extent), dealing with minor problems/glitches (health issues, bathroom breaks, pointless bickering) and getting the feel of how to approach the material, which is inconsistent since each day I'm someplace new in different schools with different smells and different students, something like a quasi-Bohemian.

My "ease" in the classroom, and familiarity with some of the class' setups (I have subbed a combine total of 36 days, some repeats), and my role, as Instructor, has allowed me to comfortably "change" the class schedule somewhat to make room for what I have come to regard as "Class Exercises" but they're less simple than the description. These "changes" are usually based on personal observations. Here is the breakdown of your average classroom: out of (say) 30 kids (an even number for personal ease), approximately six (three boys, three girls) are the "alphas," the popular ones (for either being "cooler" or "more confident" or "more attractive" or whatever limiting criteria they have running through their heads). The "Little Teacher's Helper" isn't always the most popular, but she (almost always 'she') does her chores every single day, without giving the others who want to do those chores a chance. So when I see fit I take the "usuals" out of their roles and fill their spots with others who would never get that shot - the "shyer," more reserved types, who want to do something new but no one gives them the push or has the patience to extract from their cortex those buried wishes or fantasies. Naturally, any and all changes I make are met with hostility and much mumbling and scattered conversation - the kids are always speaking to each other over their disagreements with my "changing" protocol. All of this is done solely for my amusement.

I've also started changing around the reading groups, mixing in the "better" readers with the "lesser" ones. This positively irritates the "better" readers, who whine about how "they" don't know the assignments and "they" don't belong there and how Mrs. or Mr. Instructor doesn't do it "that way." I smile and say "tough" and deliberately pace around the chief complainers and correct every minute error they make.

However, there had been occasions when my patience has been pushed to its threshold, and I brought in buckets filled with Pine-Sol and water and ordered the kids to move all the desks and scrub the floors and blackboards and walls. Days like those are usually when the children will simply not pay attention so I rationalize that if they do not want to learn they will scrub. More whiners - alpha or omega, I seriously care not - get assigned extra work, in particular cleaning off the Instructor's desk and placing everything back in their proper places - small picture albums, birthday/holiday cards, textbooks, cups filled with assorted pens, magnetic paper clip holders. Meanwhile, I sit and read my book, which I have learned to bring with me.

When I go back to Chesapeake a second time for Gardner's grade, I made sure to make Gardner the Class Leader, just because, and had him take care of the morning rituals, collect lunch money, lead in the Pledge of Allegiance, monitor the room when I went to the restroom or to my car. He is, honestly, quite pissed at me for making him do this, but I certainly feel good about it, for some devious, self-centered reason.

I have been known, periodically, when in good spirits, to completely scrap whole subjects (I let the kids vote on which they dislike the most) and replace with more interesting things to do. One particular day, I was in the 4th Grade at Proft Grade School and none of the students (27, 14 boys, 13 girls) liked science very much. So I asked what they wanted to do instead of science and some recommended a field trip (improbable), one a sing-a-long (too noisy, potentially off key/grating), another kickball (too cold), another a parade (your guess is as good as mine), another a movie (I rejected this). My final decision involved bringing them all sodas from the soda machine (this ran a dollar a piece, but I didn't mind), pushed aside all of the chairs in the room, sat on the floor and had them color in pre-drawn pictures of Looney Tunes characters taken from an activity book I bought at a dollar store and photocopied. Of all the ones I made copies of (5 total), most kids picked the one of the effeminate Bugs Bunny taunting a bound-and-determined Elmer Fudd by squeezing one of his cheeks (much to the hunter's chagrin).

Naturally, a few became agitated while sitting and coloring (I, meanwhile, read *The Sailor Who Fell from Grace with the Sea*) and I had to separate a boy and a girl next to each other because the girl was yelling at the boy for having his outstretched foot too close to her. The boy, recognizing her irritation and not-yet-aware that he is biologically pre-determined to woo the female and not disrupt her, kept it there. I had to take the effort of setting the book down, getting up and moving the boy to the left of the room and the girl to the right, by the window. Both of them complained, the girl especially, since she wanted to be near her friends, but I said I was sorry and she just pouted and looked out the window. The boy, away from the others, played with his shoelaces.

———

Preston, while I worked at my last job, had basically set-up his son as being some hell brand-on-Earth, who both looked as if he misbehaved and had, constantly. When I was able to cover his class, 5th Grade at West Hills, I was curious and anxious to see what kind of lad he actually was - you know how you create a mental image of someone and then when you meet them it almost never, ever matches up properly? I, admittedly, was tentative to have him in my class - if he was as bad as I pictured, I'd get so fed up I'd make him clean my car, for fear the little Che would lead a guerrilla assault on yours truly.

But Kyle, I found, isn't exactly a hell-brand, continuing that string of faulty mental images of others one tends to generate. The kid is, how do I say this ... both pompous and extroverted. He's just *energetic*, dramatic, lively in spurts - he's fond of large, sweeping gestures - he doesn't clap his hands, he slams them together with all the energy in his arms, producing a banging sound; he doesn't walk to the cafeteria, he *stomps*, especially on the feet of others. Yet, he isn't like that *all* the time - most of the time he's actually quiet, reading, writing, sitting still (or with his feet propped up on his desk). I'm most in awe of the sneaky, elaborate games he finds a way to pull off which involve pitting people against each other (tough to describe - but he knows how to start arguments and spread bizarre rumors and point fingers and walk away quiet and straight-faced). I don't consider this *bad*, merely unique. I'd say he's one of those love-him-or-hate-him kind-of-kid - you either find charm in the tongue-in-cheek maliciousness or get irritated by the sneakiness and scene-stealing. If I had this class for more than a few days in a row I'd probably change my opinion of him. More than anything I see it as a way for him to enliven his peers, who don't always provide him with the audience he needs. He is, for his classroom, one of a kind.

I do, of course, make a mention to him, before lunch break, when the children are slowly funneling out of the room, that I know his father and how we worked together a long time ago and how he's such a nice guy but he's far too interested in this book on manatees that he found on the classroom bookshelf.

"He said you're doing well, here. Do you like it?" I ask him. His grades, by the way, are in the B-range, which is fine, I guess.

"What?" He's too busy staring at the pictures in the book.

"Your Dad. I know him. He said you're doing well here even though he said it's a tough school." I found no evidence to support the latter claim, but I've only been here for a few hours now.

There's no response. He's just standing there, with the book.

"Do you like animals and stuff like that?"

"Not really."

"I see."

"Look at this one," he says as he hands me the text. The photograph he's pointing to is that of two manatees with their heads sticking out of some body of water near Florida, as if playing peek-a-boo.

I hand it back to him. "Neat. I was asking you before: do you like it here?"

He closes the book and flops it on a nearby desk. "Why do you want to know?"

"Just curious."

"What do you think?"

"I think it's fine," I respond.

"Me too. We should go to lunch," he says and he goes into the hall.

I follow him out. "Tell your Dad I said 'Hello.'"

"Will do, Mr. Devon."

"I appreciate it," I say, and laugh to myself.

———

Other Notes.

Number of times I had to break up a physical altercation:
One. It was between two boys in the 2nd Grade - they
entered the room in the morning already fed up with each
other due to some preexisting interpersonal
conflict/problem/argument that carried over from some
other moment in time, and after a lot of angry looks and
staring (nothing verbal) the one just got up from his seat -
in the middle of class - then the other one, and they rushed
towards each other and started pushing, back and forth, and
the pushes got harder so that their heads would actually
snap around and this escalated to slap-type hitting and
palm-thrusts to the face (the one boy almost fell backwards
over the desk to his left). I separated the two and escorted
both of them to the main office for the Secretary and
Principal to deal with. When I returned a little girl in the
front row had drawn a picture of what I thought was a dog
drinking water out of a baseball hat but she explained that it
was actually me sitting at a desk and talking. The two boys
never returned.

Most desired activities by the children besides recess:
trivia-related games, poker, wandering around the
hallways, starting rumors, using classroom computers. The
last is easily the most cherished, and kids bicker with each
other as to who has what time limits to use it. I end the
bickering by pulling plugs. I am not interested in serving
as referee.

Strangest question I got asked: So few to choose from. The only good one: a longhaired kid in the 7th Grade asked me if my shoes were made by Hermès.   It turns out his sister works for them or someone that sells them someplace in New York.   "No," I told him, "but if you can get me a pair, I'd change some of your grades for you. Size 11." He told me he'd work on it.

Number of "stars" or "stickers" or "checkmarks" or "prizes" I have issued for the Instructor-invented Skinnerian positive reinforcement-type system in some classes: Zero.   They are not my "real" students - I should not be in charge of giving them such things.   The one 3rd Grade boy, after being forced to answer a question and actually getting it right, not-so-delicately indicated to me that Mr. Somebody puts "checkmarks" on a chart in the front of the room next to the student's name each time he/she gets a right answer.   Ten checkmarks and you get a "star," ten "stars" and you win a trip to Thailand or something.   He went hissy when I told him I wouldn't and he replied by saying he'll tell Mr. Somebody and Mr. Somebody will give it to him.   "You do that," I said.

Best advice I received in the time I've been teaching and ignored: It came from the Assistant Secretary at Governor King, who said that you should "Start the day off strong and no-nonsense, and gradually ease up as the day goes by."   I *have* thought about it, but just never exactly followed it, as it sounded like something that came out of a manual Ms. Nicolette read from during the Seminar.

Approximated percentage of young girls (mostly first through eighth) who unnaturally dye their hair blonde that are not naturally blonde, all grades: Approximately 70% (+/- 5%)[*]

Number of young boys (first through eighth): 12% (+/- 2%)[*]

[*] These numbers were actually tallied via head count, and the final numbers you see there are the averages. I could do a complete and total breakdown of the numbers and compiled data, but that is unnecessary. Take my word for it.

20.

For December, work has been delayed - Joan the Sub Caller hasn't had as many slots for me (which she actually apologized for but I told her not to be so silly and I asked if anyone had complained about what I was doing and she said "not that I know of"). No matter: I've already reasoned that *the idea of youth is a drug. It's also, simultaneously, a plague.* In a matter of two weeks all I have is one day to cover - that's all, leaving me a lot of time to stay home and read or drink pot after pot after pot of green tea, which, according to the "Science" section of the local paper, helps reduce my chances for colon cancer, leaving me open for heart failure, stroke and Alzheimer's which they don't have tea for yet but I'm sure the Japanese are working on it, as we speak, in their dark, subterranean laboratories.

Frankly, I'd rather not work during the whole month of December. It's my favorite month - not just because it contains my birthday, which is today (thank you, thank you), but because of the feeling it emits, as if the weather has a personality and its presence could influence your thinking and behavior. Less light, more quiet - these are the ideal conditions that distinguish winter days from those boisterous summer ones, overblown with chatter and chaos and energy and haste. December, in comparison, carries the air of stagnant water and muted breezes, slower driving, colder mid-afternoons.

Earlier today, I bought myself a cake and a new pair of shiny, dark brown Hermès shoes (I never did work in that kid's class who spoke of them again). They are ridiculously priced, but a splendid gift for my feet. The amount of money in my savings account is decreasing slightly, but that's because I've cut down on a lot of *excessive* needless spending, this being the most expensive thing I've paid for in the past, oh, it's been a while. Anyway, I'm worth it.

Right now I'm enjoying my time, eating the cake piece by piece, making sure to carefully carve off and dispose of the sugary/icing parts and flipping through *The Screwtape Letters*, which, strangely enough, smells like oregano, even though there don't appear to be any spilt spices scattered near or on the bookshelf I took it from.

There are three phone calls: Davis and Sterling each call, one right after the other, some twenty minutes apart, and wish me a Happy Birthday, which I accept, and they both inform me that they have gifts for me when they see me next. Sterling invites me over to his place to have dinner with Annie but I decline and say I'm busy (he doesn't ask "Doing what?" and I am grateful, because I do not have a satisfactory answer). The third phone call comes from Mom, who invites me over for cake and whatnot. I tell her Sterling's having a party for me and I can't - perhaps some other day. She says she bought a small cake and that they would only toss it out if I didn't come over. She doesn't mention the office.

"We won't keep you from your busy life," she tells me, "just stop by a minute, say hi."

"But I have to be somewhere else soon."

"Oh," she says, and then nothing.

I sigh. "Who is there?"

"Just me and Dad, who else would be here?"

"How about tomorrow?"

"What time do you have to be somewhere else?"

"8."

"It's 6:30 now."

My shoulders drop. "I'll be there now."

"We'll be waiting."

I need to rehearse my story, while driving over, about work, relationships and matters involving life - I don't want to worry them terribly.

———

Both of them appeared to be in ideal health and spirited moods, and we shoot the breeze for only about 45 minutes. They ask about work and whether or not I went for any promotions and I said come the New Year I'll be moving up and they both seem pleased. They inquired as to how I was getting along with Davis and Sterling and what we've been up to and I said 'same old' and they laughed as if they knew what that meant. During the conversation - in their living room, with the gas stove hissing and emitting orange and the television set playing some hockey game - Mom offers me some eggnog Uncle Bill made but I decline, as I always have. Dad honestly surprised me - he seemed in good spirits, was surprisingly verbose and volunteered a lot about what he's been up to at his practice, funny anecdotes, gossip about people I know of. Mom, as expected, was quiet and reserved. Neither mentioned that I forgot to stop by Thanksgiving a few days ago, which passed by without me even giving it much thought.

I leave at a little after 7:30, and give them both a hug and say goodbye, neither saying to call - because they know I rarely do - and mention that if I get a chance, to stop by Christmas day, which I said I'd try to do. I thanked them for the deep blue Burberry coat with a leather collar that was my birthday present - quite a nice gift.

As I drive away I put my arm out the window and flap it about, all the while honking like a madman.

May nothing but happiness come to them.

21.

On the following Friday night, I get a phone call from Davis inviting me to have dinner with him, Sterling and Eric at some restaurant Eric's girlfriend/fiancée works at, and apparently can get us free food and such, and they, according to Eric, have the best Manhattan Clam Chowder on fucking Earth, which I think is some sort of lure to get me to go. I tell him no, sorry - I have (inventing some mystery illness) a slight bout of dizziness that creeps up out of nowhere, and I got it looked at and am taking Antivert for, but at the same time I'm still a little nauseous and don't want to risk it. He doesn't ask again, or question the 'truth' behind the 'me-going-to-a-physician-for-once' story, but just tells me to rest and I tell him I will.

Since I have had only a little bit of work lately (a day here, a day there) I continue to spend more and more time in my apartment - days on end, without leaving or speaking to anyone. I find, when in situations like these, I am actually more "productive" than usual. Now, when I say "productive," I don't mean to infer I'm constructing anything artistically praise-worthy - on the contrary - most of the time my energies are misdirected and nothing meaningful gets accomplished. But I have been working strong on my sketches and "journals" which are sketchy and incoherent but are still there, on paper. I focus less on the sketches than the journals, as the former frustrates me more than the latter. So "productive," for me, means, "doing what I like."

I stay up until about 1:30 AM proofreading the introduction to some short story I wrote (please do not ask for details - the piece requires *expansive* revisions) and go through a small tin of Ginseng Peppermint tea. The night is exceptionally cool - how beautiful, I think - and I open up the balcony door about three inches to let the mist funnel in and fill the room up with some much-needed purity. To compensate I put on my heavy green-and-black striped bathrobe (that is sullied in only one tiny way: a small coffee stain rests on its left sleeve), and double wrap myself in two blankets - one baby blue, the other white - and lay down on my mattress and allow the briskness to tickle my face - while the rest of me remains piping hot. I proofread and add to the story until my body and primal parts of my brain get the best of me and I fall asleep.

Now, I don't know *what time* it is when the phone call comes and I really have no idea where I'm at - the ringing causes me to leap up and start scrambling in the dark, stumbling over the blankets wrapped around me and my legs, over the crumbled papers and books and stencils and colored pencils to get to the phone. The room is revoltingly cold now - I had forgotten to shut the balcony door - and I'm shocked I slept through such torturous conditions.

When I pick up, my voice is crackling and harsh, as expected. "What?"

There's a long pause and I repeat myself, only louder. "Oh

Jesus-" a woman's voice says - she's breathing heavily.

"Mom? Is that you? What's going on?"

"Christ, Devon ... he-he's dead. He and...."

"Mom? Mom? Hello? Who the fuck is this?"

"It's Marie. I, I heard from Davis' mother, not, uhh, not too long ago and she said," and she breaks off, breathing, coughing, sniffling between breaths.

"Who? Marie? Marie? What happened?"

"They found the car, somebody saw it in the-"

"What? Whose car?"

"Davis' car. I just can't. I can't believe it."

"What *happened*?"

"They found Davis' car not too long ago ups-upside down in the Dumont Canal, all of them - they all," she stops talking and coughs hard, in-between what sounds like dry-heaving.

I'm not sure I believe what I'm hearing. "So ... he's dead?"

"Yes."

"Sterling - was he in there?"

"Yes."

"He's ... dead too?"

"Both of them and someone else in the backseat." She's trying to inhale but taking it in big gulps, as if undergoing an asthma attack.

"Are you okay?" I ask.

A soft "yeah" can be heard.

"Who else was in there? Did anyone survive? Eric was with them too."

"Eric wasn't in there."

"So they all drowned, right? In the canal? Or was it a car accident?"

"I don't know the details, all I know is they found the car in there, upside down, and all of them dead."

"Well, what - what time is it?"

"I *knew* I shouldn't have let him out tonight. I just *knew* it." She continues crying - bawling, now, even louder than before.

I start looking around for my clock, but can't see it from where I'm sitting, and am too cold to stand up.

"I'm so sorry," I tell her, "but how did you know to call me?"

"Because Davis' mother told me you weren't in there and Davis said before he left that you were sick."

"I see." A pause. "Do you need me over there? Does she need me?"

"No."

Another long pause, a couple of sneezes by me.

"I can't believe it," I tell her.

"Neither can I."

"Were they drinking?"

"I don't know," she says, "Davis shouldn't have because he's on allergy medication."

After this there's another very long pause in which I think of the *right thing* to say, but I figure the break gives me sufficient time to absorb everything. I find myself just sitting, huddled in my cloth igloo, the white blanket covering my head and ears, in the corner, with the phone pressed against the wall and my head pressed against the phone.

"He invited me to go with them," I say.

"I know."

I don't want to say it's lucky I didn't, although this could be obviously inferred.

More silence, more crying.

I wonder whether or not they got a hold of Davis' sister or parents, who the third party is, what on Earth caused the car to - according to what she said - flip it over in a canal. I picture them trapped inside the vehicle, gasping for air, clawing to get out, which I probably shouldn't think of, but do anyway.

"Listen," I say, "why don't we just ... go and, hang up for now and if you hear anything or find out anything else, please call me if you can." I don't feel like pressing for questions now, and give her time to calm down.

"Okay."

"Are you sure you don't want me to come over?" I'm volunteering.

"I'd rather you didn't," she tells me.

"Well then please, just ... relax."

"You too," she says.

"I will. And thank you for calling and letting me know."

"It just ... doesn't *feel real*," she offers.

"I know. You should take some Valium. For your nerves."

"I did."

"And?"

"It's not working yet."

Pause.

"Well, please, remember to call me with more information. Keep me posted on everything."

"I will."

"Take care, okay?"

"Okay."

"Bye."

Click.

I put the phone back on the hook and rest my head against the wall. I feel too drained to walk over to check the clock in the kitchen or shut the balcony door, which is open but a sliver.

I close my eyes and shiver myself back to sleep. *Deus ex machina*, I recall, in purely literary terms.

22.

It is 11:21 when I arise, which is alarming, because I expected more phone calls (or perhaps I slept through them?). I don't know how many people Marie had to call or notify, but I'm assuming she has her hands full. To ensure that there won't be any potential phone calls, I unplug the jack from the wall and toss the entire phone - wires and all - out the balcony door, where it drops X feet and collides with the sidewalk, causing its plastic casing to shatter like shrapnel. I also shut the balcony door for the first time - the room is a tundra.

I prepare myself a cup of honey & lemon-flavored black tea to try to kill off the incoming headache and throbbing pain - I associate with resting in sub-thermal temperatures - and eat some cereal and leaf through Dickens' *A Christmas Carol* which I always swore I'd try to read *around* Christmas time but never got a chance to. After breakfast I shower, again, for about 45 minutes, get dressed and drive to the local library where I go to Floor B0 and start off by grabbing some random books on the shelf (one's on gardening, another cultural anthropology, yet another on divorce), going over their words and the ideas they want to convey, the real-life divorce-related arguments (one lawyer cites a case in which the husband and wife were so furious and uncompromising that they resorted to arguing over - among other things - an orange extension cord), the *Do It Yourself* guides on herbs. I spend a great deal of time re-reading the chapters in the anthropology book regarding 'myths' and 'mythemes' in other cultures, none of which I honestly "get" or comprehend but at least I am putting forth the effort to try to learn.

As to why I'm in the library: I felt I needed a change of scenery. I also didn't want to be around my home in case strange people would come by to ask puzzling questions dealing with my acquaintances, where they were, past behavior, or what I know about last night or have to speak to anybody about practically anything I don't have a well-prepared answer for. I'm not interested in speaking to family or people from high school, attending viewings, funerals, masses, ceremonies, after-ceremony meals (which are merely gossip festivals), having to witness weepy-weepies and flailing and unrestrained lamenting. I remain semi-curious as to who the third person was in the car, and interested in some of the exact technical details (ex: how did the car end up in the water? did it go off a bridge a la the cinema? did it skid off the road? were they drinking? did it just flip off the side? I always had considered it a light car). Something will probably be in the paper.

So curiosity takes me again and I start scouring for material on autopsies and forensic pathology (not the liveliest subjects - I agree - and not something that typically captivates me). I look up "Drowning" in the Index of this one text I find. There are five pages listed, some of which seem obvious, some not so. Essentially, there are two different types of drowning: "wet" and "dry." "Dry" drowning is much less common than "wet" drowning, and is called so because no water enters the lungs - the "drowning" part is actually from a "laryngospasm," which is a constriction of the individual's airway by water finding its way into the throat. "Wet" drowning comes from liquids getting into the lungs. The book fails to state which is more "common."

A few more random things: most drowning instances are due to accidents and lead to brain death (lack of air).

Autopsies can't "prove" the individual died by "drowning" - such a label is utilized after other possibilities (for cause of death) have been gone through and systematically eliminated. The book is ten years old, however - have any new developments been made? Or is this the be-all and end-all?

At 4:30, when the library is getting ready to close, I leave and drive around my apartment building to scan for Marie, parents, strangers, police and the like (honestly, I don't know *why* the police would be there, but you never do know). While I don't see any nearby, I opt to go out for dinner, at the Nascosto, an Italian restaurant that's a little expensive but delicious, or so I recall reading in the "Food/Travel" section of the local paper. Since 4:30 (roughly) is still time when people are at work, and since the restaurant first opened at 3, there are not any people inside, other than the Hostess, a squat curly-blonde woman with a polo shirt, black pants and shimmering ruby lipstick surrounding her mouth. I request the booth in the far back - and she obliges. It isn't as if I am inconveniencing anyone else.

A lot of people make "ambience" out to be an important factor in choosing where to eat, but I have never grasped onto the concept (does the placement of tables and seats maintain digestive harmony?) or is it simply a matter of "making the place look clean and interesting?" Clean I need, interesting I can do without - I can always ignore the Betty Boop clock and bobsleds nailed into the wall, or, more generally, *kitsch for kitsch's sake.*

Within the Nascosto, there are simply a lot of oil lamps and dim lighting and framed prints of gondolas and children running and old men sleeping placed sparingly about, a floral arrangement on this wall, a rectangular mirror on that. Nothing hurts the eye, but nothing "wows" it either. A large rectangular fish tank is in the absolute center of the room, with only two fish inside, each swimming on the opposite side of the other. The one is a bluish color, the other, slightly yellow-orange (perhaps marigold).

My waitress is Misty, a 20-something brunette who's wearing a short-black miniskirt and a button-down blouse with the cuffs undone and hanging loose from her arms, something like dangling shackles. Her hair is tussled but clean, and pulled back and held together by a cloth band.

I order a glass of water and Mussels Marinara (with angel hair pasta), and she jots that down on her notepad with a black Bic pen using her ring-laden fingers covered with sparkling purple nail polish. I ask her if the place is always this empty and she tells me yes, sort-of, then she looks around, then I don't know, then *hmmmm* - all in sequence. Because today is Saturday, she says, it is a bit strange, but it may have something to do with the weather and the forecast predicted it might snow a little later on.

She leaves and I wait a short while for my meal - in the meantime I notice an elderly couple step in stacked to the hilt with winter apparel - him with a large brown overcoat and matching hat (no feather in it), her with a suit-type red jacket with black buttons. I approximate their respective ages to be in the 70-75 range. They hang their coats up in the cubbyhole with hangers in the right hand corner by the entranceway and are quickly seated. They peruse the menus they're given, not looking at each other or saying anything. When Misty goes over to their table, she orders first, then he, Misty takes all that down, leaves the two sit there, menus whisked away, silent, glancing left and right at the walls and decor and at me, adjusting various articles of clothing (pants, shirt, socks, stockings) or body parts (hair, ears, nose - especially the nose, which I have noticed in the past is a big area for hand gestures to be focused on, particularly when I am around - people are always rubbing it, touching it, scratching it, holding it, placing their index finger perpendicular underneath it or horizontal along the one side or covering it up completely with several - sometimes two, sometimes three - fingers).

I get so caught up in watching them ignore each other (it's almost as if they're dining alone but just so happen to be stuck in the same square area) that I'm startled when Misty arrives with my dinner on a large white plate covered with cheese which I did not ask for but thank her all the same.

When I finish I pay the bill (the meal is $14.75 plus tax and a three dollar tip) I notice two more people are seated, eating and chatting in another corner. The old couple has since received their orders and are carefully and cautiously consuming it, one trembling forkful at a time, as if the meal were sleeping and they dared not disturb it.

I drive towards my apartment building, continuing to scope out the territory for suspicious cars. It is past 6 PM, and I figure it's still early for me to make my way inside so I park the car in an alleyway across the street and down about a hundred feet and lock the doors and let the seat go back and rest a bit. At 9 PM I leave and go park where I normally do (in front, where I have a special pass) and pace up the front steps slowly. No sign of anyone, anywhere - good, so I can take a shower and listen to the radio.

I plan out what to do Sunday, when the library is closed: spend all day at the mall (not even remotely convenient or the place you'd typically find me, but I have to go someplace) drinking coffee and looking at pants.

23.

On Tuesday I see *the* article in the newspaper at the library (which I've made my temporary hideout) and read through it for details and such. There were no articles in Monday's paper for some reason. As always, I've edited it for easier reading, omitting what I took as the unnecessaries, the spaces indicated by ellipsis points I added:

THREE DROWN IN CANAL

On Friday night, three individuals, two male, one female, were found dead in a red Pontiac Camaro upside down in the freezing cold waters of the Dumont Canal. After having run into a fence on Washington Road, the vehicle flipped forward and plunged, roof downwards, into the canal.

The canal's depth ranges from seven to eight and a half feet deep.

...

The three who died Friday were Sterling Harrison, 26, Catherine Windsor, 25 and Davis Klein, 26, who was the driver.

According to the police, the victims were attending a Christmas Party. All three left together, although no one indicated where they were headed.

...

On Monday, Coroner F. P. Ruhe completed autopsies for all three victims, and came to the conclusion all had died of drowning.

...

The driver of the vehicle, Klein, had an extreme blood-alcohol ratio of .18. The blood-alcohol level for Harrison was .19 and Windsor .07.

...

Possible explanations for the drowning varied. The cloudiness of the water, due to dirt and debris, the frigid water and the levels of intoxication most likely lead to panic and fear while underwater. The individuals could have opened the doors or possibly lowered the windows to get out. The water pressure was not enough to make escape impossible. Police report that all three were tangled in their seatbelts, which also hindered their escape.

...

Funeral arrangements ... [etc.]

The omitted parts contain what I discern is mostly hearsay and speculation and talking heads, none of which I care for and don't feel the need to relay to you. What I'm still reeling from is how the third passenger was not Eric, but Catherine. Sterling's eyes may not have fooled him the one Friday night so many months ago. The article says nothing about her, gives little of her background or much of anything.

The article also makes no mention of Eric.

The article also makes no mention of whether it was "wet" or "dry" drowning.

Finally, I will not be attending funerals, no matter how piqued my curiosity.

———

Days pass and nights come, mornings shine brightly and middays beg for body stretching and sky-gazing, noting every bird and tree and cock-shaped cloud that floats by. The cold air doesn't bother me much as of late - as long as I'm bundled to the nine's and have on my Burberry coat - providing soothing insulation (I do wear this to bed sometimes and leave the balcony door open). I pass several days simply going to the library or strolling around my block, watching, taking in the smells, uneager to call up the School District and report I "lost" my telephone and what-do-you-have-for-me, content with letting other Substitutes deal with the useless simulacra. I do admit to not exactly being accustomed to my revised schedule - days on end, sleeping late, staying up late. There is a certain amount of freedom to it, for sure.

I have not seen nor heard from any unwanted guests for the past few days, which I am quite grateful for. If I felt I needed *assistance*, I would have found a way to get it. Some ailments can be cured within, I read.

To waste time I sit and read or create word collages out of newspaper words, pasted into my Sketch Book and colored in with scented markers I bought at the local super store for office supplies that has Christ-knows every single object in the world for work-related needs and *whew* how convenient they are in one warehouse-type establishment. Oh, along with the markers I also purchased a $90 straight cut paper shredder, which I put to good use by dicing up almost everything in sight - I take various articles in my filing cabinet, sift through them (short-stories, essays, biographical pieces, extremist "I-Can-Change-The-Free-World" documents that are unintentionally humorous and thus labeled as 'camp,' I suppose, or perhaps taken seriously, maybe) and feed them through, filling up many garbage bags, then taking them out to the dumpster behind the Bank down the block and dropping them in.

(And the collages I made with the newspaper clippings? They had the honor of being shredded first, immediately after the glue dried.)

At times, while in my shredding fits, I'm not always paying much attention to what is being eliminated. One nice piece I find, and am startled I kept it, was a make-up note from Davis to Catherine (which he never gave her and is why I still have it), which features lines like, "... I am completely honest with you and always have been" and "You have to stop being so *difficult* all the time" [italics added]. Remember what I said before about what material sounds like when you're not in your right mind and mad or upset and what comes out of your mouth or head or fingertips comes out not as intended, but rather like utter childish *nonsense* when you read it later?

While shopping I did catch a look at the phones they had for sale - the cheap ones, in particular - but couldn't drag myself to buy another one. I watched the other people accumulate and carry, in labeled bags with fistfuls of Mall Pretzels and Mall Beverages.

24.

Christmas comes and Christmas goes, New Year's comes and New Year's goes, tiny flakes stream by and the cold continues, yet I am unfazed, and remain, seated, unmoving, by the balcony door, from the inside, looking out, wrapped in cloth, with my tea, watching nothing in particular, and entertained, for too long, by drawing flowers and smiley-faces in the parts of the window my breath has graced. The clocks have appeared to stop, the calendar inconsequential - no jobs, no endeavors, no nothing - simply unmistakable redundancy remains. For some strange reason I kind-of miss the sporadic phone call from anyone, the check-to-see-how-you-are-even-if-I-really-don't-care sort of time-waster. Just two minutes.

(But what am I saying? Like a phone call would make much of a difference to anything.)

The entire filing cabinet is now a skeleton, with featherweight drawers freed of the globe resting on their shoulders. I've also taken several cardboard containers, which I pilfered from the supermarket, filled them with old books off the myriad of shelves in my room I felt no need for (or no *drive* to tackle) and placed them outside the local library, at 3 in the morning, in return for them letting me spend time in their basement, using all day to lounge about and smell the mildew.

I have also taken various articles of clothing that I didn't want anymore, and boxed them up, took them to the Salvation Army, placed them outside the front door, like a newborn baby left on the doorstep of "expecting parents," as told in fairy tales. I felt another change was necessary, hence the "Spring Cleaning in Winter."

I have *also* taken it upon myself to withdraw everything in the bank, some six-thousand-plus dollars, and set it on the kitchen table, trying to decide why I took it out in the first place, then realizing I should probably put it back in, then figuring I should wait and let time pass and figure out where to put it all. One should not have that much money lying about.

There is nothing keeping me tied down, nothing telling me 'you cannot do X,' so I'm here, left with a multitude of options, ways to go. I do not want to stay here, so I decide to create a plan, and intend on mentally mapping it out.

––––

The Life Decision (with the alternative title, "A Plan For Me") that I devise comes to full realization at 12:16 PM on a gray Wednesday afternoon, a day chock-full of overcast and frosty wind. It involves several preliminary steps before it can be set into action, which I have charted on one of the few pieces of paper remaining in my apartment. I assure you, this is excessively well thought out (for those that assume it is a *spur of the moment* thing):

<u>The Three Steps</u>

Step 1. Decide what to do with the loose cash.
Step 2. Remove all belongings from the apartment
except furniture (reason: too heavy,
run risk of personal injury like hernia)
Step 3. Deal with the car, the vehicle identification
number (VIN) and personal belongings.

––––

Step One's resolution arrives in my head sooner than I thought - I take all of the thousands of dollars on the table (from my savings account) and toss it into a large manila envelope, with a hand-written note that merely reads:

This is a donation: keep it, use it, don't ask

I seal it, place eleven stamps on it and mail it to the American Cancer Society, the address of which I found in the phone book. Why them? I don't know. I was going to mail it to my parents, but then they'd just wonder what I was doing, or think I received a raise. The organs of people brushing past me in public, in anonymous space, are filled with malevolent cancer, and every anonymous penny may help.

———

For Step Two, more books and more clothes get dumped at the aforementioned places (I notice, days after I've dropped off the clothes and books at the Salvation Army and the library - respectively - that they are not by the doors and hopefully taken in and made useful). I reluctantly toss out the radio I've grown to love and listen to the weather forecasts on, and stuff it into a garbage bag and toss that into the dumpster, along with unrelated items I scavenge from the kitchen, such as cleaning supplies, stencils, markers, scissors, hot mitts, all the forks except one, all the spoons except one, as well as all of the plates (I have paper), cups (again, I have paper), the IBM typewriter (goodbye), the rest of the manila folders and envelopes and stationary I have, as well as all of the stamps, random trinkets (a hockey puck, a baseball hat with the Pistons logo on it, the New Mexican dried red pepper decoration), food products (cans of soup, boxes of rice, several boxes and tins of tea) and, finally, the paper shredder itself. I use up five boxes of garbage bags to toss every scrap of anything found in the place. I would love to see the next bill the bank gets from the Sanitation People.

All I'm left with is a duffel bag that I purchased from an Army surplus store (paid for it with cash), several pairs of socks, several pairs of underwear, a toothbrush with the handle snapped off (every gram of weight can feel like an eternity after a day of walking), Colgate toothpaste, a razor for shaving, a knife from Farberware, a crowbar, a hooded sweatshirt, long underwear, a pair of sweatpants, two pairs of Dockers (both dark green), several long sleeve shirts, a bar of soap, an enormous plastic jug that I fill with Centrum Multi-Vitamins, a blanket, my Hermès shoes and the heavy Burberry coat.

———

For Step Three I go outside, to my car, with a screwdriver and crowbar and sharp Farberware knife and unscrew the license plate, scratch the registration stickers off the windshield, remove all the contents from the glove compartment (including car registration and operational manuals) and rip them up into tiny pieces and place them into yet another black Hefty bag. I take the crowbar and pry out the registration plate on the dash of the car, right by the steering wheel (it is aided by the thin blade of the knife). I then pop the hood, lurch through the contents until I find the engine, and proceed to pry that one off as well, squeezing my bony fingers inside and around all of the tubes and metal. After I do so (and bend the knife considerably), I toss that in the black bag, along with the antenna (which I snap off) and rearview mirror. I use the bent knife to slash the seats in the front and back, tearing out the stuffing and cushion-y material and place them, too in the bag, along with floor mats, loose change, the flashlight from the "break-in" that I forgot to take inside, an umbrella and a few loose scraps of paper, take all that, along with the knife and the crowbar, and throw them into the garbage. I get in the car, drive it six miles until I get to a run-down part of town, park it in the middle of nowhere, by an out-of-business restaurant, lock the doors, take the keys and walk six miles back to the apartment.

Once I get back I pack the duffel bag with the necessary (and sorted) items I've left behind and not trashed, don later after layer of clothing to battle the elements, leave a note on the kitchen table reading:

"Dear Whomever,

I am leaving because I feel like things aren't working out exactly, so rather than tolerate repetition and the sham of living the same day over and over again, am altering personal goals. I feel I have stayed in one spot long enough. I am leaving you with your worries in this sweet cesspool. Good luck."

… and set my apartment key on top of the piece of paper and do a final check through all the cupboards and drawers and in the bathroom and all around to see if I had forgotten to pitch anything. I realize Seth's bike is still in the closet in the hall - he can always get that later.

I pass his door, and Amy's on the first, as I pounce down the steps for the last time. I fail to hear sounds from either apartment. I can only hope that the next tenant who takes my apartment is as cooperative as I was. May nothing but happiness come to them.

And so, all three Steps have been completed. Success.

———

I begin my "Excursion" by simply walking, duffel bang slung around me (its thick strap itching to form a permanent notch in my shoulder(s)), with my ski mask sucked to my face, my layers of clothing (sweatpants on top of pants on top of pants on top of long underwear; sweatshirt over button-down shirt over button-down shirt over T-shirt), my coat, my gloves, and walk towards the highway, leading North. I don't exactly know where I'm headed - and on several occasions actually chuckle, to myself, at how ridiculous I'm being - but tirelessly press on, convinced this is the route that is best for me for this specific moment in time. I've read it somewhere, and it applies to me: I have grown old in places where I never meant to stay.

I pace through town, through traffic, down cracked sidewalks and trashcans and bottles of generic seltzer water rolling around the pavement, tussled and pushed by the wind. I stomp through the grass, which is light green, sometimes brown, and short. The wind continuously bothers my eyes.

Come nighttime, I duck down an alleyway and surround myself with garbage cans and such to "hide" me from people driving by, and also protect me from the weather. I use the duffel bag as a big pillow to rest my upper body on. There has been perhaps no more adequate time for me to sit and think of where to go, where to head. Answers flip about, ranging from Canada and then fly over to some other country after taking some small job and getting up just enough money (I could have done this before, but decided that was simply too easy). But some irrepressible probe in the deep recesses of my head tell me that everything there is just like here, they're just the same, that the scenarios are all the same, that only the language is different. I find myself with more questions and more doubts.

My goal is founded in a dream of mine to "start from scratch," to literally become *the* Consummate Vagrant.

25.

Countless strangers have drifted past me (and I past them) often glancing at me from the corners of the sockets of their eyes. I can't tell you what they're thinking, although to be able to do so would certainly benefit me (and, definitely, everyone else). Knowing where we stand with one another could be a wonderful-terrible thing.

I've found my way to the highway - or some highway extension - and it does, indeed, lead north. I continue to, days on end, trudge along, the earth rising to meet each tired step and exert strain on my ankles and knees and legs and lower back, while the duffel bag weighs on my shoulders, arms and back. Highways are significantly less interesting than country roads or urban roads - only speeding cars, flying gravel and the constant fear of being run over from behind accompany you on your journey. After a while, like everything, you get used to it, and occasionally spot something visual on the side - mostly loose change someone has thrown out their car window (the heft of which most obviously weighed a ton in his/her pants/jacket pocket) or random trash or road kill (deer, squirrels). Some people honk as they pass by me at alarming speeds but I pay little attention. I've seen Police Officers in their cars or on motorcycles whiz by, but they never stop me (I question whether or not walking on a highway is legal if you have no legitimate purpose to do so - broken down automobile, for example).

Once it starts to get dark I immediately look for an off-route to saunter down and rest for the night, behind some building or by bushes or by gas stations or truck stops where, if lucky, they have showers for truck drivers that are unbelievably cheap and allow me to freshen up, warding off days of sweat and stink and unregulated time.

For general drinking water, the best resource is from bathroom sinks, which also happen to be good interim wash-up spots to get gravel and soot out of my hair as well as wash off my gloves and face, brush my teeth and shave (lathering up with the bathroom soap).

Meals tend to be a different story - I've discovered I've spent several days at a time swallowing Centrums and water left and right, hoping to keep the necessary supplements nourishing my body, which is constantly being tested. I'm often able to purchase a bag of chips with the highest amount of fat from a vending machine if I've saved up enough change. I must admit that I do go many nights with sharp pains in my lower abdomen and painful, throbbing headaches, but since I know why I have them I am not concerned.

I stopped counting the days a while ago. I'm guessing it's February by the frost every morning on my clothing and blanket and the tops of the metal garbage containers, although it could very well still be January.

———

I eventually end up in a small city - with red-brick houses and stone buildings and fancy street lights that curve and twist in every direction (yet the light still faces downwards), all of which are placed parallel to each other as they run down the street in perfect symmetry. There are various shops open but sealed shut to yield off the inclement weather (beautiful, wondrous flurries, filling my eyes with a splendid white, erasing everything else, slowly). This is actually a treat for me - I decided to take a small break from my excursion and peruse the area (the highway's redundancy has gotten to me a little and I wanted a visual change of scenery).

I manage to sneak into a bookstore in this town, shaking the few flakes of snow off my tattered shoes and begin to look around. I've left my duffel bag outside - I don't presume anyone in his or her right mind would want it. I've also taken off my ski mask to avoid scaring anyone inside.

Inside, the Manager, a woman, sees me and says hello, which I reply to, and she then makes some comment about the weather and how she thinks it's only going to get worse later, and I say oh that's fantastic because I love snow and she rolls her eyes and chuckles. I also tell her how deliciously warm it is in the cozy shop, and she informs me of exactly what number is on the thermostat inside (81°) versus outside (28°). It feels like a sauna. I can't spend too much time in here or I'll have to start taking things off.

I run across a book on skiing for beginners and I immediately think of Davis and Sterling and how they would always try to coax me into accompanying them all the while saying how it was "just like ice skating," which they failed to recall I was also bad at, and almost tore my arm off grabbing the railing to avoid slipping and falling. You'd think now, in retrospect, I'd feel bad about not tagging along, but I do not.

I poke around more shelves all of which are poorly organized. When the Manager - in her 40's, mauve turtleneck sweater - goes to the back room I stuff two paperbacks into my coat sleeves (one's on the abortion debate, the other's on kinesics). When she comes back, I keep an eye on her, but she pays no attention to me - she's busy neatly rearranging the shelves of books on rickety makeshift wooden racks that reach up to the ceiling and extend horizontally as well, all of them too big for the constraints of the tiny shop and making maneuverability a bit of a problem. I stumble over a cardboard box of bargain books in the left-most aisle (it has a sign declaring that everything in there is on sale for a dollar) and accidentally knock some loose entries about. She sees this and tells me not to worry about it - that she'll get it - but I insist and straighten up anyway, out of courtesy. I was looking around for more books to take but figure two is enough, say goodbye and walk out to the snow and ¼ inch of powder on the ground.

26.

As of late the Centrum has been running low and I have been unable to find much food, so my stomach pains and headaches have gotten much worse. I have recently fallen prey to small bouts of nausea, dry heaving and dizziness (all of them being interrelated), which subside after a little while of not moving my head or body.

(I still obstinately refuse to eat from garbage bins or beg for money.)

As a matter of fact, out of personal amusement, I have constructed a makeshift cardboard sign for myself to carry along with me and wave about (or, if feeling too ill to walk, sitting on benches or steps and holding it in front of me). In homage to the art world, I wrote this statement on the top of a pizza box with a broken pencil I picked up off the ground (the words accented with an almost-dry yellow highlighter I scavenged):

I am redeemable
because of my youth.
Give me nothing
Move on

My hands have started trembling to the point where it's literally hard to look at them. I also have severe back pain from the days of lugging around the duffel bag with me, my shoulders ache, my knees burn, my neck delivers shocks of discomfort to my head when I rotate it. I continue to brush my teeth and shave when I head into bathrooms but haven't really showered in a long time - there aren't any YMCA's or truck stops to do it at. I contemplated breaking into someone's house to freshen up and change clothes and wash and eat oh-so-quickly, and then head back out again, but decided I didn't want to disturb anybody or cause them any emotional distress. Think of it: being robbed is the ultimate violation of safety. Where can we be without the thin illusion of safety? Or comfort?

So all I'm left to do is walk and watch, sit and watch, sit and stare, examine all through my two portholes, my two black abysses, both set deep within my skull (and being pushed further back by time itself). I refuse to stop walking, to grow impatient, to chastise myself. As for myself, as for right now, I am surrounded by no one: the area is free of traffic, trees, those terrible blending faces. What a wonderful feeling. I have only myself, alone, here, *desireless*. And in my soul, there is something strong, unbending, unrelenting. You can't see it, and neither can I, but I can feel it, and always have, and always will.

It is my prayer for you.

www.ingramcontent.com/pod-product-compliance
Lightning Source LLC
Chambersburg PA
CBHW060140130626
46556CB00006B/2427